The Stacks
The Complete Series

KATIE DEVOE

To my lovely Danny

PART ONE

CHAPTER ONE

Tristan Everett's mouth dropped open in surprise when he caught sight of the familiar beauty leaning over the desk, her brow furrowed in concentration. It couldn't be. He blinked, but sure enough, there she was. Melanie Potter. He hadn't seen her in nearly two years, but she wasn't the type of woman a man forgot.

For four agonizing months, she'd sat in the front row of his senior seminar, watching him intently with those big green eyes of hers. It had been pure, delicious torture. Melanie Potter was a rare beauty, better suited for a Dutch painting than real life. Pale skin and long auburn hair hanging loose around her shoulders. He'd almost wished she'd dropped the class. Because Melanie Potter wasn't just beautiful, she was untouchable. And he'd wanted to do more than touch.

It didn't matter that the university strictly prohibited relationships between students and professors. There were lines Tristan just wouldn't cross. Risking his reputation for a reckless fling with a student was definitely one of them.

No matter how many times he'd been tempted to do just that. Instead, he'd been forced to fantasize in private, imagining what could have been if circumstances were different. He'd found relief either alone, in the shower, or with one of several women willing to satisfy his needs without asking for more in return.

He couldn't believe it was really her, but there she was, just as breathtaking as he remembered. He leaned against a bookshelf and crossed his arms over his chest, watching with interest as she lifted her arms above her head, stretching like a long, lean cat, completely unaware of the effect she was having on him.

He glowered in irritation, feeling himself grow hard in his pants. What the fuck was wrong with him? He felt like a horny teenager, unable to control his reaction to the sight of a beautiful woman. At thirty-five, he was too old to let his dick do the thinking. For a split second, he considered turning around and finding some other deserted corner of the library where he could grade papers in peace.

Her full, pink lips moved as she read to herself, her voice inaudible above the hum of the air-conditioning and he couldn't resist. She wasn't his student anymore. There was nothing explicitly wrong with what he had in mind. He pushed off the bookshelf and strode towards her, determined to at least talk to her, aware that he was about to step over some invisible line.

He perched on the edge of the table, watching with amusement as her lips continued to move in silence. God, she had beautiful lips.

"Do you always do that?"

She jumped in surprise. "Holy shit," she exclaimed, yanking out her earbuds. When she looked up, her eyes widened in recognition. "Professor Everett? You scared the crap out of me."

"I think you've earned the right to call me Tristan," he said smoothly. "How are you? And what in God's name are you doing here?"

Melanie laughed, pushing her hair out of her face. "I'm visiting a friend. I thought I'd check out the library."

"Students don't usually come here unless forced."

She shrugged. "Taking advantage of all the alumni privileges my tuition bought me. Anyway, I begin grad school in the fall and I thought I'd get a head start on my reading."

"Here?" Tristan was on the admissions committee for the English Department and there was no way her name would have slipped past him unnoticed.

"No, Princeton."

"In English?"

She shook her head again. "Comparative Lit."

"An equally profitable career choice."

She grinned. "Honestly, I don't think I'm cut out for anything else. Now, for five years, someone is going to pay me to read." She shrugged. "I'll figure the rest out later."

He leaned back, crossing his arms over his chest, considering her briefly. It wasn't the answer he'd been expecting, that was for sure. Most students who passed through his classroom seemed more interested in financial success than in actual learning, a thought that depressed him frequently.

Melanie tilted her head back as she looked up at him, her lips parted and he couldn't help but imagine what it would be like to have her looking up at him with that same curious expression as her lips closed tight around him.

Tristan had to drag his eyes back to hers, hoping she didn't notice.

"I'll let you get back to it," he said, pushing off the desk with a nod. He knew he was making a mistake before the words were even out of his mouth, but he couldn't help himself. "If you don't have anything better planned tonight, let me buy you a drink."

He held his breath, watching as Melanie's expression shifted from puzzled to excited.

"That would be great!"

He nodded again. "I'll see you outside at eight."

With that, Tristan turned on his heels and strode off, trying to put as much distance between them as possible. He was going to regret this, but all he could think about was getting her naked in his bed.

Mel continued staring long after the door slammed shut behind Tristan Everett, her heart beating wildly in her chest. She couldn't believe it. No fucking way had Professor Everett just invited her out for a drink.

She wrinkled her nose, unable to stop from laughing. She'd secretly hoped to see him on campus, maybe catch a glimpse as he strode purposefully across the quad, distracted and gorgeous as usual, but she definitely didn't expect to run into him, much less that he'd ask her out for a drink.

She'd had a thing for Professor Everett from the moment she set foot in his senior seminar and saw him standing by the chalkboard, scowling. He'd looked around the classroom before abruptly telling them that he wouldn't tolerate slacking off. Anyone looking for an easy grade before graduation was free to walk out. Then he'd stared out at them, silently daring one of them to get up and leave. No one did, but by the next week, more than half the students had dropped the class.

Mel wasn't one of them, though she'd considered it. Not because she was scared of the coursework. She knew she could handle that. She liked a challenge and appreciated professors who wouldn't put up with bullshit. What she didn't know was if she could handle sitting in the same room as Tristan Everett for four long months. Even scowling, the man was gorgeous. He was tall, with a lithe physique and unruly dark hair that he was always pushing out of his eyes. And god, those eyes. Dark and intense. They reminded her of Turkish coffee. What was the expression? Black as hell, strong as death, and sweet as love? That seemed to sum him up perfectly. Tristan Everett was gorgeous. And intimidating. The fact that he was cold and aloof did nothing to temper his sex appeal. If anything, it just added to his air of mystery.

Every Wednesday for four months, she left class dazed and feverish, worried he'd notice her embarrassing schoolgirl crush, but he never gave her a second glance. Professor Everett would storm out the moment he dismissed them. A few times, she'd seen him joking around with students in the hallway after class, but never with her. He'd always been perfectly civil, but that was it.

So why was he being so nice to her now? She bit her lip, trying to stop from grinning. The thought crossed her mind that maybe, just maybe, he was attracted to her. But she dismissed it quickly. Tristan Everett was way too good-looking to be single. And anyway, even if he were, New York was teeming with beautiful women who'd be more than willing to keep him warm at night.

She let out a sigh. If nothing else, tonight would give her something to fantasize about during those lonely nights at Princeton.

CHAPTER TWO

Tristan paced outside the library, checking his watch impatiently. He already regretted his impulsive offer. If he'd had her number, he would have cancelled. Made up some lame excuse. A last minute departmental meeting. A visiting colleague. Anything to get him out of having a drink alone with Melanie Potter. Because now that he'd thought about it, he realized he had no fucking idea what he was doing in inviting her out and uncertainty didn't sit well with him. Checking his watch, he realized she was late.

Any earlier reservations disappeared when it occurred to him for the first time that she might not be coming. Maybe she'd changed her mind, realizing that the last thing she wanted to do was have drinks with her stuffy old professor. Not that he was stuffy or old, he thought huffily, but that was probably how she saw him. The thought was depressing. Almost as depressing as the possibility that she'd forgotten.

Tristan clenched his jaw and glanced at his watch one final time, resigned to the fact that she wasn't coming.

He'd go home, open a bottle of wine and try to put her out of his head. He could always call Emma. She was usually free and more than willing to spend the night tangled in his sheets. But the idea of Emma, or any woman who wasn't Melanie for that matter, left him indifferent. He sighed and took one last look at the library, holding his breath as the doors opened. And then he saw her. Wind ruffled her long auburn waves, and she looked around, squinting as she tried to locate him. She pulled her khaki trench coat tight around her.

He stalked across the square, coming to a stop in front of her, close enough to catch a hint of her perfume. For a moment, they both just stood there. The wind whipped her hair around her face and he was tempted to brush it behind her ear.

He registered a flicker of confusion in her large, green eyes and clenching his jaw in irritation, he leaned down and pressed a light kiss to her cheek, feeling her soft skin beneath his lips. It was only a second, but for that brief moment, it was as if the world stood still and all he could feel was her warm skin, infusing him with heat, the smell of her perfume making him lightheaded.

He stepped back, startled. "Let's go," he said gruffly and started towards Amsterdam Avenue, Melanie falling in step beside him, the heels of her boots clicking loudly against the paving stones.

Le Bistro Noir on Frederick Douglas Boulevard was far enough from campus that there was little danger of running into anyone they knew. Tristan often went there to get away from the congestion on Broadway, the constant chatter of college students and the dreaded possibility of running into another member of the English Department. He'd bring a book and sit, undisturbed, for hours, a luxury in a city like New York. He chose the restaurant without thinking, but now that they were seated, Melanie's beautiful face illuminated in the flickering candlelight, he realized his mistake. This was the type of place you brought a date, not a former student.

"Have you been here before?" he asked, glancing down at the cocktail menu and hoping she wouldn't read too much into it. He wanted to sleep with Melanie, not date her, and the last thing he wanted was to give her the wrong impression.

"No, I'm more of a boxed wine sort of girl," she answered, laughing and the sound of her easy laughter made his shoulders fall with relief.

"Tell me you weren't one of those drunken screaming girls at the Heights," he said sarcastically.

"Can't say I'm much of a drunken screamer," she said, brushing her hair from her face. "I didn't go out much in college," she added hastily.

He shifted uncomfortably as the waitress arrived to take their order. When Mel ordered a glass of pinot noir, Tristan decided they might as well share a bottle.

"Are you hungry?" he asked before the waitress could tuck her pad into the pocket of her apron. Melanie bit her lip before shaking her head. Tristan's eyes narrowed as he tried to decide if she was just being polite.

Finally he shrugged. "I'm starved. We'll also have an order of pate and the cheese plate," he said. "I hope you aren't a vegetarian," he added, handing the waitress his menu.

"Nope, not after a brief stint in college."

"How does one end up having a brief stint as a vegetarian?"

Melanie shrugged, spreading her napkin on her lap. "It was sort of a bet with a friend. To see if I could do it."

"And could you?"

Melanie laughed freely. "I think I lasted a month. It was brutal. A woman cannot survive on falafel alone."

Tristan felt himself smiling. "I'll try to remember that."

By the time the waitress arrived with the wine, Tristan felt more in control of the situation. He could do this. They'd have a pleasant evening, catch up like old friends, and then he'd wish her good luck with grad school and that would be that. Simple. Easy. He just wished she'd stop biting her lip.

The waitress poured him a sip of wine and he waved his hand impatiently, assuring her it was fine.

"What are you doing back in New York?"

Melanie looked up, hesitating a moment before answering. "I broke up with my boyfriend and needed to get out of Seattle to clear my head," she said softly. "We lived together."

"I'm sorry," he said, taken aback by her candid response. "I'm sure that's very difficult."

Melanie shrugged, but the way she avoided his gaze, he could tell her indifference was merely an act. If they'd lived together, their relationship must have been serious. He frowned, curious to know just how serious. The fact that he felt a flicker of hope, knowing she was single, made him feel like a monster and it didn't help when he saw her shift awkwardly in her seat. What sort of man actually felt joy at hearing a woman just went through a difficult breakup, he thought with disgust.

"These things happen," she said breezily. "Anyway, a friend is letting me crash with her until I go down to Princeton."

"How long are you here for?" he asked, hoping to steer the conversation towards safer territory.

"Five days. I need to find an apartment and get my life in order before I start work."

"Then I guess it's lucky I ran into you today," Tristan said, surprised to find he actually meant it, but his innocent remark seemed to take on a sudden weight when Melanie's face broke into a dazzling smile.

Tristan looked away, focusing all his attention on spreading pate on a piece of bread. Without thinking, he handed it to her and picked up another piece.

"Where does your friend live?"

"On the Lower East Side. The apartment's a shoebox but the location is great. Unfortunately, Carrie's boyfriend works from home so it's best if I'm gone during the day."

Tristan frowned. He could imagine what a recent college graduate's apartment on the Lower East Side looked like and just the thought made him cringe. She was probably sleeping on a futon surrounded by pizza boxes and empty beer bottles.

"It's really not bad," she added, smiling. "And anyways, it gives me an excuse to spend more time at the library."

Tristan thought guiltily of the guestroom in his apartment and the large, unoccupied bed. For a split second, he considered offering it to her. It wasn't like anyone was using it. But just as quickly, he dismissed the thought. If Melanie stayed at his apartment, there wasn't a chance in hell he'd let her sleep in the guestroom. If he let her sleep at all.

Melanie lifted her glass to her lips, and Tristan noticed, not for the first time, how beautiful her wrists were. Delicate and slight. He'd always had a weakness for wrists and he had to shake his head, desperately trying to dismiss the vision that crossed his mind: Melanie's body, perfect and naked, except for the black satin that bound her, her rich auburn hair fanned out on his bed.

Tristan's erection strained painfully against his pants and he had to dig his nails into his palms, praying the pain would blot out the tantalizing image.

"What were you doing in Seattle?" he asked, refusing to dwell on the thought of Melanie Potter in his apartment or his bed.

"I was interning at a publishing company, editing cookbooks."

They continued talking, their conversation surprisingly light and easy. Tristan was curious to hear more about what she was studying and Melanie asked him about his research and before they knew it, they'd finished the wine and Tristan was ordering the check.

A cold wind whipped Mel's hair around her face as she struggled to button her jacket. Next to her, Tristan had his hands shoved in his pockets as he glared off into the distance.

"Is everything okay?"

"Everything's fine," he answered without so much as looking at her.

She frowned, suddenly worried that she'd been wrong in assuming they'd actually had a good time.

"Are you ready?" he asked tersely.

"Thanks again. You really didn't have to," she said as

they started up 110th Street. If nothing else, this would make a bizarre story to tell Carrie when she got home later. Carrie knew all about Mel's ridiculous obsession with Tristan Everett after putting up with her talking about him incessantly during college.

Tristan hunched his broad shoulders against the cold. "It was my pleasure," he answered smoothly. "I really am glad I ran into you."

His husky voice made her nipples bead. She'd spent the entire night trying not to stare at him like a creepy groupie and now she worried that maybe she'd given him the wrong impression. She sighed. It was too late to rectify the situation now. She'd blown her one chance with the man she'd spent years dreaming about.

They continued in silence past Morningside Park towards the subway on Broadway. Tristan stalked ahead, his long strides making it difficult for Mel to keep up. She was too busy staring at the pavement to notice Tristan stopping abruptly and she collided with the hard wall of his chest.

"Whoa," he said, cupping her shoulder with his hand to steady her, sending an unavoidable thrill through Mel's body, making her stumble back in surprise.

"Are you alright?" Tristan asked, his dark eyes narrowing on her in concern.

Mel struggled to laugh. "I'm fine, I just didn't see you."

"Are you sure?"

Mel nodded. "Yeah, I'm fine. Just a little clumsy is all."

Tristan looked away, as if just now realizing they were standing on the corner of 110th and Broadway, mere steps from the 1 train. Mel held her breath as she watched him, her eyes wide and hopeful. His gaze lingered on the subway entrance before he turned back to her and straightened his shoulders, a newly determined look in his eyes.

"I live around the corner," he said suddenly. "Would you like to come up for a drink?"

CHAPTER THREE

Tristan unlocked the front door to his apartment, holding it open for Melanie as she slid past with the agility of a dancer. Now that she was here, standing in his living room, so close he could touch her, he wondered what the hell he was thinking. But then she glanced over her shoulder, giving him a rare smile that he could feel all the way to his toes, and he knew exactly what he was thinking. He didn't care how many unspoken rules he'd have to break, he wanted her and he'd make it happen.

"Let me take your coat," he offered, watching her slip out of her trench. She was wearing a simple wrap dress, tied at the waist, that clung to her curves in a way that left little to the imagination. He hung their coats while Melanie walked to the large windows overlooking the Hudson River, and beyond that, the twinkling lights of New Jersey.

"What would you like to drink?"

She glanced over her shoulder. "Whatever you're having is fine," she answered, her voice light and musical, before turning back to the window.

He found an open bottle of red wine in the kitchen from the previous night and poured them each a glass.

For a long moment, he leaned against the doorway, watching her. He could watch her all night. She had to know what he had in mind inviting her back to his apartment. She wasn't naïve and she'd accepted without hesitation, but he still worried that she'd walk the moment she realized his true desires. There was just something about her, an air of otherworldly innocence that worried him at the same time that it called to him. He didn't want to corrupt her, but he wasn't looking for a relationship, either, and there was no point in beating around the bush. If she expected lovemaking and romance, he wasn't the man for her. Not when what he really wanted, more than anything, was to fuck her raw. To take her with such wild abandon it left them both panting and speechless and yearning for more.

He sighed, knowing he'd find out soon enough. The thought that she might walk out terrified him, but he wasn't interested in leading her on, in letting her think he was ever going to be the type of man interested in romancing or making love. No, he needed a woman who understood his limitations and accepted him for who he was. Letting his eyes linger over the seductive curves of Melanie's hips, he just prayed she was that woman. Because the idea of letting her walk out now, when he was so close to finally getting what he wanted, set him on edge.

His cock strained uncomfortably against the confines of his pants, making him impatient and he took one final sip of wine before setting their glasses on a side table. Wine could wait, right now he couldn't.

He took a step closer, coming to stand behind her,

amazed that even in heels, she only reached his chin. Without thinking, he placed his hand on her hip, pulling her against him, pleased by the way she acquiesced. His manhood twitched impatiently as it ground into her ass and he leaned down, inhaling her intoxicating scent, and placed his lips to her neck, eliciting a sigh in response.

Tristan could feel her frantic heart beating against his chest where their bodies came together as she struggled to remain perfectly still. God, being this close to her was torture. Delicious torture and that made him itch for more.

Gradually, she relaxed into him, her whole body soft and pliant, and he let out a sigh of relief. It didn't take much to imagine her beneath him, the way her tightness would grip him before gradually relaxing to accommodate his girth. He tightened his grip on her hip.

When he was certain she wouldn't shrug him off, he spun her around roughly until she was facing him, her face upturned as her lips formed a surprised "O". The look in her eyes, that twinkling excitement made him acutely aware of her readiness .

"Professor Everett…"

Before she could finish, his lips were on hers, kissing her fiercely, possessively, the way he'd always imagined kissing her. He wanted to kiss away that name on her lips. The fact that she referred to him as "Professor" sent a wave of conflicted arousal crashing over him. He wanted her to see him as only a man.

He'd deal with any repercussions tomorrow, under the clear and sobering light of morning, but for now, he needed to taste her. Her soft lips parted in invitation and he took full advantage, letting his hands roam her back as he kissed her, cupping her ass through the sheer material of her dress as he pulled her flush against his hard body. She moaned softly as her hands found his hair, holding him fast. She kissed with an intensity that nearly brought him to his knees, making him realize there was no way he would let her walk.

Fuck, if he wasn't careful, he'd end up fucking her right here against the living room windows. He tugged her lower lip between his teeth before leaning back, keeping his hands firmly planted on her hips. He had no intention of letting her go.

"You have no fucking idea how long I've wanted to do that," he groaned, struggling to catch his breath.

Her lips curved into a playful smile. "Me too."

God, the way she was looking at him, it took all of his earthly willpower not to hoist her into his arms then and there and carry her off to his bedroom.

"I've wanted you from the moment you walked into my seminar," he admitted.

"I almost dropped the class."

"Why?"

She looked up, her eyes large and earnest. "Because I couldn't concentrate around you."

Mel squeezed her eyes shut, trying to escape the intensity of Tristan's gaze. The way he looked at her, his dark eyes warm and inviting…it was so much more than sexual desire. It was as if, for the first time in her life, a man could see all the way into her soul.

Finally, she opened her eyes and stared up at him. God, he was gorgeous. His unruly hair was a mess around his head from her grabbing hands and his lips were parted in invitation. Power emanated from him and she could feel the wetness gathering between her legs as she struggled to think clearly. She didn't want this to stop but she knew she had to ask.

"Are you sure this is a good idea?"

His lips curled into a wry smile. "Yes. I am," he breathed onto her neck, his hands running over her skin in a silken caress, making her nipples harden to sharp points. Every time he looked at her like that, she imagined what it would be like to have him inside her, making her wet and anxious.

"You're no longer my student," he continued, lifting his shoulders in a slight shrug. "And I know exactly what I want."

All she could do was nod in response as her heart thundered in her chest, unable to comprehend that this was actually happening. Tristan Everett was meant to be one of those lifelong fantasies, a missed opportunity that was never really an opportunity to begin with.

"But if you don't," he said, lifting one eyebrow, daring her to disagree, "I can always get the doorman to flag you a taxi. It's your call. What do you want?"

His loaded question hung in the air between them but Mel didn't have to consider her answer.

"I want this," she said almost stubbornly. Something about the way he was looking at her, with careful calculation, made her think she should be careful. That Tristan Everett wasn't going to be an easy man. But she dismissed the thought.

"Good." He shifted subtly, drawing himself to his full, powerful height. "You're here for five days?" he asked slowly.

"Yes."

"And your boyfriend. He's out of the picture?"

Mel nodded in surprise. Tristan had a way of making everything else fall away until there was nothing left but the two of them. She knew she should feel guilty about wanting another man so soon, but right now, she couldn't think of anything except Tristan touching her, having her, taking her. His hands on her hips were driving her wild, fueling the need that had been simmering just below the surface all night.

"Yes. It's over," she said breathily.

Mel saw a flash of something in Tristan's eyes. "I'm going to be direct with you. I plan on fucking you for the next five days. And I want you to submit completely. To be mine and do as I say without question.

"I'm not into pain and I will not hurt you. I plan on making you come over and over again. I will pleasure you in ways that you've never experienced. I will tie you up and have you totally at my mercy. I love spanking a woman until her ass is red and burning and then fucking her. I don't want a girlfriend and I don't make love. I need you to understand that. While you're here, I will fuck you, repeatedly, but that's it."

Mel blinked, feeling an unexpected tug at her sex as she considered his words. And yet, she wasn't surprised by them. After four months in a class with him, she knew that Tristan was a man who oozed power and control. Why should it surprise her that those same qualities that had drawn her to him initially would extend to the bedroom?

He watched her carefully, his jaw tense as he waited for her response. The way he was looking at her, the way his eyes burned into her, made her shiver. But not with fear. She nodded slowly, feeling the sharp edge of desire curling low in her belly.

"Okay," she said slowly, as the corners of her lips turned up in a smile. A look of relief passed over him and she wondered if he'd really been worried she'd say no.

She took a step towards him, wanting more than anything to feel his touch on her fevered skin, but he stepped back, maintaining the distance between them. "I should call you a taxi."

"What?" she squeaked.

"I want you to think about what I've said. I'm serious, Melanie. I want you. But on my terms. I need to know you'll do anything I ask. No questions. You have to trust me. I won't hurt you, but I will push you to your limits. If there's anything you won't do, you need to tell me. Because when you're mine, I expect to have you whenever and however I want. If you don't think you can handle that, there's no point in this going any further."

Mel shook her head. "You've got to be fucking kidding me." She was primed and ready and he was seriously telling her to leave. She shook her head again. "I'm not going anywhere."

His lips curled into a flirtatious grin. "I assure you, I'm perfectly serious. But I want you to think about it. I don't want you making a rash decision."

"This isn't a rash decision," she protested, once more stepping towards him, but he placed a hand on her shoulder, stopping her.

"It is. I want you to think about this. Alone. You can't make this decision when I'm touching you and I swear to God, I won't be able to keep my hands off you if you stay."

"You're horrible," Mel said in frustration.

"No," he said with fierce determination. "I want to ensure you are completely comfortable with my terms. Because once we start, there is no turning back. Come on." He dropped his hand from her shoulder. "Let's get your jacket. I'll walk you down."

Melanie stared after him, knowing there was nothing she could do to change his mind. What he'd said didn't change a thing. She wanted Tristan Everett, the whole man. If that meant submitting to him…She brushed her finger over her bruised lips, smiling at the memory of his passionate kisses.

"This isn't going to change my answer," she said coyly. Tristan gave her a dark look before helping her into her jacket.

He leaned in, placing a gentle kiss to the base of her neck, making the hairs stand to attention. "I hoped you'd say that, but I still want you to think about it," he whispered.

"You don't play fair," she said with a throaty laugh.

"Who said anything about playing fair?"

His words made her sex clench with anticipation. If she was this turned on from a few kisses, imagine what it would be like in his bed?

Outside on Riverside Drive, Tristan hailed her a taxi. "If you decide to take me up on my offer, meet me in the stacks tomorrow at two," he said.

"And Melanie, wear a dress."

CHAPTER FOUR

At six am, Tristan slipped out of bed, too agitated to sleep. Thoughts of Melanie had kept him awake most of the night, tossing and turning as he imagined all the dreams he'd finally be able to put to rest. He quickly changed into his running gear and headed to Riverside Park. There was nothing like a punishing run to calm his usually agitated mind.

But the calm never lasted long. Running was a drug his body had sadly grown used to.

He checked the time. A little before two. No matter how impatient he was to see Melanie Potter again, he wanted to make her wait. That was, if she'd even come. Last night, he'd given her a lot to think about and he wouldn't be the least bit surprised if she'd realized she wasn't interested in what he had to offer. He'd seen the way she looked at him, had felt her body mold to his. There was no doubt in his mind that she wanted him. His only fear was that he'd come on too heavy. But five days wasn't a lot of time and he didn't want to ease into this.

No, he wanted Melanie and he wanted her on his terms. So he'd given her the opportunity to walk. Now he just worried she might have taken it.

He sighed and strode into the library, barely glancing around as he made his way straight to the stacks. He hoped she'd be there. He'd lain awake all night, thinking about her, fantasizing about her. Five days wasn't a lot but it would give him more than enough time to explore every inch of her beautiful body. If she was willing.

The air conditioner hummed noisily as he pushed open the door to the stacks and inhaled the comforting smell of old books. He couldn't explain why he'd insisted on meeting her here, but it felt right.

When he turned the corner, his eyes landed on Melanie and he breathed out a sigh of relief. She was actually there. And she was perfect. The way she pursed her lips in concentration. The way her beautiful hair cascaded around her shoulders. He couldn't wait to wrap his hands in that hair, fisting it as he pulled her into his kiss.

His long legs carried him easily across the distance that separated them. Tristan placed his hands on Melanie's delicate shoulders, relishing the feel of her bare skin beneath his palms and the startled sound that escaped her lips.

"I wasn't sure you'd come," he murmured.

She looked up at him with those beautiful wide green eyes. "Of course I came."

His lips curled into a satisfied smile. "And you're wearing a dress."

"You told me to," she said easily. As if obeying him was already ingrained in her, a need so basic she hadn't realized it existed.

Tristan leaned down, breathing in the scent of her, floral and feminine and perfectly fitting. "I teach in an hour. That gives us more than enough time to get better acquainted." His words were a dark promise, making Mel's body stiffen in surprise and anticipation. She looked around nervously, relieved to confirm they were still alone, but that could change at any moment.

"Here?" she asked unsteadily.

"Here." Tristan let his hands drop from her shoulders. "Stand up and turn around," he demanded brusquely.

Mel struggled to her feet, pushing aside her chair and turning to face Tristan. His lithe body boxed her in against the desk, highlighting her vulnerability. Her nipples puckered in response to his appreciative gaze.

"You look stunning," he said, reaching out to brush a lock of her auburn hair behind her ear with surprising tenderness. "I've been looking forward to this moment all day. If you hadn't been here," he paused, dismissing the thought with a shake of his head. "I would have been very disappointed."

The way he said disappointed sent a shiver through her body. Mel licked her lips, trying desperately to keep her eyes on Tristan's. He watched her internal struggle, his lips curling into a sly smile.

"What do you have in mind?" she asked shakily.

"You. God, you're all I've been able to think about. I want you. All of you. But for now, I want to taste you," he said slowly, drawing out his response, letting it wash over Mel's senses. "I want to watch you struggle to maintain control. I want to see the moment you give in and you lose it." His perfectly composed tone was so at odds with his erotic statement. "Take off your panties and give them to me."

He crossed his arms over his chest and leaned back, watching her intently to gauge her reaction. This was it, he thought. She'd either do what he asked or she'd realize she couldn't. He held his breath.

Mel bit her lip nervously before lowering her eyes, her long lashes brushing her pale skin. Carefully, she reached under her skirt and slowly pulled down the lace panties she'd worn specially for him, stepping gracefully out of them and handing them to Tristan. He smiled and lifted them to his face, inhaling deeply. Mel blushed, knowing he'd be able to tell how excited she was.

"Good girl." He tucked her panties into the back pocket of his pants.

He pulled her close, pressing his lips against hers in a powerful kiss that robbed her of her senses. His lips were demanding, forcefully taking her, marking her as his. If she'd had any doubt as to the type of lover Tristan would be, she knew now.

Never breaking their connection, he snaked one hand down her side, caressing her soft curves, before slipping under her skirt, finding her wet and swollen. He ran a single finger along her slick folds, feeling her tremble in his arms.

"That's it," he coaxed, sliding his finger into her, feeling her tighten in response. "I can't wait to fuck this greedy little pussy of yours, but that will have to wait."

Mel whimpered, suddenly afraid that he'd leave her here, panting with need, but Tristan gave her a reassuring smile, easing her worries. "Don't worry, baby. I'll take care of you." Another finger joined the first as he fucked her in long, leisurely strokes designed to drive her crazy without ever bringing her to climax. Mel leaned against the desk, letting her eyes fall shut.

"Eyes open." His fingers stilled inside her, making Mel clamp down in desperation. Hesitantly, she opened her eyes, blinking slowly as she took in the sight of him. His whole body radiated power. He was beautiful and completely in control.

"I want you looking at me when I make you come," he said, his gruff voice the only indication of his altered state. "I want to watch you come apart."

Mel shuddered when his thumb found her clit, roughly circling her tender flesh. Her chest heaved as she struggled to keep herself upright, struggled to keep her eyes on Tristan's, knowing instinctively that even the slightest disobedience would cause him to stop what he was doing. Her belly quivered and her lips fell open in a silent plea. Tristan smiled down at her. She was so close. So close that she actually whimpered when he stopped stroking her clit.

"Not yet," he warned, watching her eyes widen in distress as he continued to fuck her with long, leisurely thrusts of his fingers. "I want you begging when I finally bring you over the edge."

His savage words stole her breath away and she knew he had every intention of keeping his promise. If he wanted her to beg, he'd get her to beg.

"Tristan," she started. Her whole body was on fire while her mind struggled to accept what was happening. "Please," she heard herself begging, the reedy sound of her voice unfamiliar even to her ears.

"Please what?" He lifted one eyebrow as he looked at her.

"Please."

His fingers stilled inside her wet cunt, making her curse in frustration.

"Please, Tristan. Make me come." She stared at him, her eyes wide and pleading.

Mel whimpered when Tristan's thumb once brushed her clit, the touch intimate and teasing.

He leaned in, crushing his lips to Mel's. When he finally pulled back, she stared up at him, her eyes glazed with desire. "I think you can do better than that," he said deviously.

Mel shuddered. "Please," she pleaded, all dignity obliterated by need. "Please. I need you. I need to come. Please make me come."

Tristan's lips curled smugly. "Baby, you don't know how sexy it is to hear you beg."

Tristan dropped to his knees and pushed her skirt around her hips, spreading her legs until his lips found her clit. His tongue flicked against her, accelerating as Mel struggled to keep her eyes locked on Tristan's. She wouldn't give him another excuse to torment her.

Every muscle in her body tensed, starting deep in her belly and spreading like delicious warmth through her limbs.

She screamed out, no longer the least bit concerned that someone might hear her. She shuddered around his mouth, coming apart at the seams as Tristan relentlessly lapped against her quivering sex, watching her lose control. There was nothing more breathtaking in this world than having a beautiful woman come in your mouth.

"That's it, baby," he whispered and stood, as one final quiver wracked her body and she collapsed against his chest, her shallow breathing labored.

When she finally looked up, Mel watched in horror as Tristan pushed his fingers into her mouth, making her taste herself on him. Her lips closed over them as she imagined her lips closing hard over his cock, suckling him.

"Tristan…"

He placed a kiss to the top of her head. "I know."

Tristan finally pulled back, cupping her face in his hands. "I have to go, but I need to see you later. This is just the beginning, Melanie. Be at my apartment by 7. The doorman will let you in. When I arrive, I expect you naked."

With that, Tristan kissed her, once again proving his dominance and ownership, leaving Mel gasping when he strode out of the library stacks.

She sagged into her chair, her mind reeling. *Holy fuck.*

CHAPTER FIVE

Mel's hands shook as she unlocked the door to Tristan's apartment. Beyond the windows, the sun dipped below the horizon, filling the apartment with a blinding, orange glow. She locked the door behind her, struck by the sudden silence of the apartment. Tristan hadn't mentioned when he'd be back. All he'd said was that he expected her naked. She trembled at the thought, knowing that he'd have some punishment in store for her if she disobeyed. Something told her it would be just as erotic an experience, though likely less fulfilling, but she wasn't in the mood to find out. Not when their time was so limited. Not when she'd been on edge since their earlier encounter in the stacks.

Her orgasm had done nothing to lessen the need she felt. No, Tristan had guaranteed she'd be primed and ready for him.

She wandered into the living room, letting her eyes trail over the magnificent view of the Hudson River below. The way it sparkled in the setting sun. It was breathtaking. A lone sailboat made its way lazily up the Hudson, leaving ripples in its wake. Finally, as the sailboat disappeared from view, she peeled her eyes away and glanced around the living room. Last night Tristan hadn't given her an opportunity to look around, but now, she wanted to see everything. To understand the man who lived here. The man who had ruthlessly brought her to climax in the library this afternoon and who had all but promised so much more.

Low bookshelves lined the walls, their shelves exploding with books, while framed art reproductions hung on the walls. The room was comfortable and yet, impersonal. Decorated in an almost haphazard way that gave the impression that the person who occupied it cared little for material things. There were no framed photographs. No souvenirs from travels. No sign of the man who lived here.

The thought that he occupied this space without really living here made her inexplicitly sad.

When she finally looked up, it was a quarter past seven and she knew she had to get moving. Tristan expected her naked and she had no intention of disappointing him.

Slowly, she pulled her dress over her head, carefully folding it before placing it on the couch. She stood there in nothing but her bra, flushing at the sudden memory of Tristan shoving her panties into his pocket. Had he taken them out when he was alone in his office?

She'd never done anything like this before. Had never stripped bare to please a man. Had never been with a man as demanding as Tristan. Her sexual experiences had always been tame and confined to the bedroom. And this sudden departure had her tingling with excitement and trepidation.

But if she were honest with herself, she'd have to admit it turned her on. The unexpected eroticism of standing there, alone, naked. The fact that she had no idea what to expect.

Though the apartment was pleasantly warm, her hardened nipples strained painfully against the lace of her bra. With a deep breath, she reached behind her, releasing the clasp, freeing her aching breasts. She let her bra slide down her arms and fall to the floor.

She crossed her arms self-consciously over her chest as she looked around, trying to decide where Tristan wanted her. The sofa faced the windows, so he wouldn't be able to see her when he walked in. There was also the armchair, angled towards the foyer and the front door. If she sat there, he'd see her the moment he opened the door.

With nervous care, she arranged herself in the chair, her legs pressed firmly together as she fought the urge to cover breasts with her arms. No, he wanted her fully exposed to him. On display.

She dragged her hand over her erect nipples, feeling them strain. She was so turned on, so wet, so ready. How long would he make her wait? Five minutes? An hour? The thought sent a shiver of excitement down her spine and she let her hand flutter low across her belly until it found her sex. He'd make her wait. She was sure of it. To put her on edge. To establish his control. She shook her head, letting her hair fall artfully around her shoulders as she stroked her slick sex, unable and unwilling to stifle her moan.

It felt like an eternity had passed when Mel finally heard Tristan's key turning in the lock. No looking back now, she thought, letting her legs fall open.

Jesus, she was stunning, Tristan thought, kicking the door shut behind him. He'd expected to find her fully clothed and sitting on the couch. Prim and proper. He would have been disappointed, but it wouldn't have mattered. It wouldn't have taken him long to get her out of her clothes.

But there she was. A vision. Her luscious auburn hair spilling over one shoulder, covering her breast. Her skin flushed with arousal. Her legs parted to let him admire the damp curls between her thighs. He may have touched her in the library, may have buried his head between her thighs, but this was the first time she'd let him look at her fully naked. And it took his breath away.

Class had been unbearable. Whenever he pushed his hair from his eyes, he caught a whiff of her on his fingers, making him insanely hard, and yet he found himself repeating the gesture though it was unnecessary. He'd been forced to lecture from behind his desk, something he never did. But today, it was necessary.

"You can't possibly know how perfect you look," he said slowly, watching the color bloom in her cheeks. Fuck, even the way she blushed turned him on. "Don't move. I'll be right back."

He strode into the kitchen, determined to find something to drink. If he wasn't careful, he'd take this too far, too fast. Something told him she wasn't nearly as experienced as she wanted him to believe. The way she blushed whenever he looked at her. Like his obvious attraction embarrassed her. Like she wasn't accustomed to being desired. It didn't make sense. Her ex-boyfriend was an idiot for not lavishing her with praise.

He wasn't worried about her inexperience. In fact, he liked the idea of molding her to his whims, teaching her to please him exactly the way he liked. The way he needed.

So far, she hadn't balked at any of his requests, eagerly obeying him, but he didn't want to push his luck. Excitement coursed through him as he hadn't felt in years.

Tristan found a bottle of red wine beneath the counter and opened it quickly, pouring them each a glass, impatient to get back to the woman waiting for him in the other room.

Mel looked up to see Tristan entering the room, a glass of wine in each hand. He came to stop in front of her and she could feel his heated gaze like a long caress against her skin. She felt flushed, feverish, out of control. She'd imagined this moment countless times but never quite like this, never with her naked while Tristan merely watched. Every fiber of her being screamed for her to cover herself but she didn't. She wouldn't.

"Here." He thrust the wine at her, which she took thankfully. His free hand trailed along her cheek and down her neck, coming to a rest on her shoulder. She took a nervous sip.

"I could spend all night looking at you. Admiring your perfect body. Watching the subtle changes that my gaze provokes. The way your breath hitches and your skin flushes."

Mel swallowed hard, her skin burning with awareness where his hand touched her, and when she breathed in, she could smell him. The subtle spice of his cologne. It suited him perfectly.

"That's cruel," she managed to get out.

A boyish grin lit up Tristan's face. "I can be very cruel when I want," he responded, his words teasing. "But not tonight. Tonight I want to explore every inch of you. I want to watch you come over and over until you're hoarse from screaming my name." He paused, letting his words sink in. "I want to feel your sweet pussy grip me like a vise as I fuck you long and hard. Later, I'll tie you up and have you any way that I want, but tonight, tonight we'll start slow."

Mel laughed huskily. "You consider this slow?"

Tristan took a sip of his wine before responding. "I could have had you in the library. I could have had you last night. I saw it in your eyes. The way you responded to me. You would have done anything I asked."

Mel averted her eyes, suddenly embarrassed by the truth in his words. There was no denying it. She would have done anything he'd asked and more.

"Look at me, Melanie."

She looked at him through her long lashes. "Mel," she said finally.

"Excuse me?" His brows came together in confusion.

"Mel," she repeated. "Only my father calls me Melanie."

"Mel," he dragged out that one syllable, feeling it in his mouth, testing it out. It suited her. His hand danced across her skin, finally cupping her breast, feeling its full weight in the palm of his hand. It fit perfectly. Its shape and weight exquisitely balanced. His thumb brushed her already straining nipple, and she subtly leaned forward, her body granting him permission as her mind continued to struggle against the knowledge of his control.

Unable to resist the temptation, he pinched her nipple ruthlessly, watching her face to gauge her reaction. She jumped, surprise emanating from her eyes and her lips dropped open in silent protest but she didn't move away. Didn't struggle at all.

"You liked that, didn't you?"

She glared at him, her eyes suddenly wide. "Yes," she gasped.

"Good girl," he murmured, stroking her cheek gently.

She shifted restlessly, the dull throbbing between her legs making it hard to think.

"I want to taste you again. And then I'm going to fuck you. You had your chance to walk away, Mel. I promise you, I'm not going to be gentle. I've wanted you since you walked into my classroom two years ago. Now that you're here, I'm not letting you go."

Tristan's fiercely possessive words sent a thrill of satisfaction through her body ending right at the juncture of her thighs.

"I thought you hated me," she admitted, surprising them both with her candor. Tristan cupped her chin, forcing her to meet his gaze.

"Hated you? Jesus, just having you in that room was torture. Knowing I couldn't have you. Couldn't touch you." He shook his head. "You're stunning. Intelligent. Beautiful. Women like you don't come around everyday," he said reverently, dropping his hand from her face, pleased by the way she continued to stare up at him. He couldn't wait to fuck that mouth but first, he needed to taste her. Needed to feel her quivering need as he lapped her up.

"Spread your legs wider," he said, taking one final sip

of his wine before placing it on the side table and dropping to his knees. God, he could smell her arousal. Could practically taste her. He quickly rearranged himself, knowing that soon he'd be buried deep inside her, fucking her for all he was worth. But first, he wanted to bring her right to the edge. He placed his hands on her creamy white thighs, spreading her legs further apart, his eyes trained on her glorious cunt.

He inhaled deeply, letting Melanie's heady aroma wash over him. He wanted to savor every minute of this. He lowered his head, running his tongue along her seam. Her surprised gasp was all he needed. He licked her with expert attention, lavishing attention on her slick folds while carefully avoiding her sensitive clit. He wanted her ready, aching, dying for him, but he didn't want her to come. Not yet. Not until he was buried deep inside her. He kissed and nibbled the sensitive skin of her thighs, leaving tiny red indentations in her flawless skin, feeling a swell of pride. He wanted to mark her, he realized.

Mel's head fell back as she tried to focus only on Tristan before her. Her belly tensed and quivered with each sinful pass of his tongue. He was teasing her and she loved it. His tongue velvety and insistent as he laved her, the deep murmuring at the base of his throat making goose bumps appear on her skin. Her hips bucked, her body begging for more. His hands found her hips, pinning her in place as he continued, licking and biting but never touching her clit. She knew he'd make her beg once more.

"Tristan." His name was a desperate plea ripped from her lips. He lifted his head, grinning at her wickedly. He brushed a lock of dark hair from his eyes, continuing to study her. It was as if he could see all the way to her core.

She'd never felt this exposed before a man and she knew it had little to do with her physical nakedness. No, Tristan Everett could see something deep inside her, something no one had ever seen before.

He gave a disapproving shake of his head before lowering his mouth to her center, making Mel's back arch out of the chair as she tried to meet him. Finally, his tongue found her clit, sucking it into his warm mouth, making her gasp as she dug her fingers into his shoulders. He'd set her on edge and now he was going to send her over, she thought in relief. Her hips continued to buck as he eased two fingers into her hot, wet cunt, fucking her with deliberate slowness as he lavished attention on her clit.

A gentle trembling began at her core, and she clamped her eyes shut, murmuring incoherently.

Tristan leaned back, keeping his fingers still buried deep inside her as he gazed at the serene expression on Mel's face. Her eyes flew open.

"You can't stop," she hissed, shuddering.

With a knowing smile, he eased his fingers from her cunt and came to his feet. He reached out, pulling her from the chair, amused by the perplexed look she was giving him.

"I want to feel you come apart on my cock," he whispered before kissing her neck. His husky voice sent a shiver through her body. She nodded, swallowing hard, feeling his erection dig into her hip. He brushed her hair back from her face, taking her lips in a possessive kiss that made her toes clench. God, this man was dangerous. She tasted herself on him, loving every second of it.

Without warning, he lifted her effortlessly into his

arms. "Wrap your legs around my waist," he bit out as he secured her against his chest, feeling her melt into him. He carried her easily to the bedroom, throwing her down on the bed before impatiently undressing. She propped herself up on one elbow, watching with growing excitement as he tossed aside his clothing.

His body was perfect. Lean muscles and tanned skin. Without his clothes, he didn't look like a professor. He looked like every woman's fantasy come true. Too perfect to be real as he strode towards her, his erection hot and heavy against his smooth abs, his cock heavenly perfection. He grabbed a condom from the bedside table, impatiently tearing it open with his teeth and sliding it over his smooth hardness.

His lips found her nipple, sucking it roughly into his mouth, biting down, and making her scream out. Her entire body trembled. She clawed at him, trying to draw his mouth to hers. She needed him. Needed the release his tongue had promised but not delivered. He grabbed her hands, pinning them above her head.

"Don't move," he bit out roughly as he teased her entrance with his tip.

She sucked her lip between her teeth, nodding her head and then, without warning, he sank into her. Filling her. Taking her. Making her his. Tristan wrapped her auburn mane around his wrist and yanked her head back.

"That's it, baby. Take me. Take all of me," he groaned into her neck, slowly easing himself out until only his tip remained inside of her. He tossed back his head, a look of animalistic need crossing his features. "God, you feel fucking amazing."

She tilted her hips, trying to take him deeper, watching

his muscles strain at the effort of holding himself back. She could see the need in his eyes, in the way the muscles of his jaw clenched. Her cunt pulsed around him, impatient. Feverish. She was so close. He'd gotten her so close in the living room and now he was making her wait.

"Tristan," she sobbed, begging him with her eyes. He thrust back into her, filling her completely. He fucked her hard. Each thrust long and determined, bringing her closer to the edge.

"Don't move your hands," he grunted, relaxing his grip. She kept her hands together above her head, her body spread out before him as he continued to fuck her. One hand found her clit, brushing against the hard mass of tingling nerves, making her whole body spasm. Each thrust of his cock stretching her. Her eyes fluttered closed as the first waves of her orgasm took over her body, violently crashing over her until her senses were erased. He continued fucking her, his thrusts wild and uncontrolled.

As the last pulsing waves of her orgasm subsided, he grunted, losing all control as he came, thrusting again and again, until she finally felt him still inside her.

He collapsed, crushing her beneath his powerful body, the weight of him oddly comforting. Finally, he pulled out, yanking off the condom and tying it off before throwing it on the ground. He supported himself on one elbow, gazing down at her, his expression unreadable.

"Call your friend and tell her you found somewhere else to stay," he said gruffly, his expression serious.

Mel stared at him in confusion.

"I'm serious, Mel. There is no fucking way I'm letting you sleep on someone's couch when you could be naked in my bed. Call her. Now."

Mel slipped from the bed to get find her phone. After she sent Carrie a text, she returned to the bedroom to find Tristan reclining against the pillows, his expression soft and contented. He motioned for her to come to him and tucked her against his side, breathing in deeply. He kissed the crown of her head and pulled her closer, feeling her nestle into the crook of his arm. He had every intention of taking her again and again until they both collapsed in exhaustion.

Tristan stared up at the ceiling, going over the evening in his head. How many times had he taken Mel? Three, four? He'd lost count, swept up on the tangle of their limbs. Mel was spectacular. The way her body molded to his. That soft expression on her face after she came. Jesus. He couldn't imagine ever getting his fill. Couldn't imagine tiring of her.

Still, regret plagued him as he wondered if he hadn't pushed too far, asked for too much. He hadn't been gentle. He'd taken her with a wild abandon he seldom unleashed this early into a relationship.

Relationship. Tristan scowled. That word had no business here.

Mel stirred next to him, burying her nose in his chest, her hair fanning out around her. He ran his fingers down her spine.

"Mel?"

She raised her head, pushing back her hair and staring up at him through lowered lashes. "Yeah?"

"I'm sorry."

"About what?" she asked sleepily.

"I should have been gentle. I should have…" he trailed

off. He wasn't accustomed to apologizing. Or feeling the need to temper himself. Mel watched him expectantly. "Mel, this is who I am. That's not changing. I'm not changing."

Mel's brows furrowed. "I think you're over thinking this a bit," she said, placing her palm flat on his chest, feeling his steady heartbeat. "I leave in a few days. No one's asking you to change."

Her words should have eased his worries, but instead, Tristan felt his chest constrict painfully. He had the sudden urge to take her again, to drive home the fact that she was his. Only his.

The thought was unsettling.

Almost as unsettling as hearing her talk about leaving. He didn't want to think about the future. A future when she was far away. A future where he didn't get to share a bed with this amazing woman.

Banishing the thought, Tristan rolled her onto her back, his body hovering over hers as he watched a beatific smile spread across her lips.

"I don't give a fuck about the future," he gritted out. "For now, you are mine." He felt her shiver beneath him, pulling her legs up on either side of his hips, opening herself for him.

"Yours?" she asked playfully, her eyes twinkling.

"Mine." The word was a desperate whisper nearly swallowed by his lips crushing down on hers. Yes, he would make her realize she belonged to him. At least for this week.

His cock brushed against her silky opening. What he wouldn't do to fuck her without a condom, to feel her wrapped tight around his cock, nothing between them, nothing separating them.

Tristan never went without a condom. There were too many risks, too many variables he couldn't account for. But there was just something about Melanie Potter that made him want to throw out all his rules.

CHAPTER SIX

Mel knew she'd eventually have to explain her disappearance to Carrie, but for now, she wanted to hold onto the blissful simplicity of the situation. Because the moment she told Carrie, she'd be forced to face reality and admit that things weren't nearly as simple as she wanted to believe.

She came to New York expecting to lick her wounds, eating ice cream from the pint, drinking wine with Carrie, figuring out what came next. Instead, she ran straight into the one man capable of making her forget all her problems and live in the moment. She didn't want to think about what came next.

Five days. That's what they agreed to. Five days of passion and then she'd leave. It sounded so simple, so perfect, when he suggested it. But now five days seemed impossibly short.

She sighed. Her bags were sitting in his bedroom where she'd put them after picking them up from Carrie's. His spare keys were in her purse. The whole thing was just so surreal, she wanted to giggle. No, it was better to stop thinking for a moment and just let whatever would happen, happen. She'd have more than enough time to analyze it to death when she got to school.

Her phone vibrated on the desk, making her jump. There was a text message from Tristan. *How's your morning?*

She smiled. Tristan was so unexpected. When she left behind her life in Seattle, she certainly hadn't expected this. Hadn't expected him. She texted him back, letting him know she'd dropped her things at his apartment before going to the library. She felt her heart rate quicken as she waited for his response.

Are you alone?

She glanced around, feeling her skin flush, but before she had a chance to respond, her phone sounded again.

I want you to touch yourself. I want you to get right to the point where you almost can't stop and then I want you to stop. If you come, I'll know.

Mel shivered, feeling a familiar tingle spread across her sex as she re-read his words. He knew she was in the library but that hadn't stopped him before, so why would it stop him now?

Her phone vibrated again, making her start. *Text me after.*

She was wearing the same dress she'd worn yesterday and Tristan had insisted she wear nothing beneath. No bra. No panties. And now, as her sex clenched impatiently, she wondered if this had been his intention all along.

She let her hand brush across her straining nipples. All it took was a single word from him and she was turned on. Ready. Aching and needy. She'd never felt this way before and she wondered if she'd ever get her fill. If there would ever be enough Tristan Everett. She doubted it. Which only made the fact that she was leaving all the more painful.

Mel rolled her nipple between her fingers, feeling it all the way to her sex. She didn't want to think about Tristan, but she hadn't been able to get him out of her mind since they'd run into each other. Hadn't been able to think about anything except him. Fucking her. Taking her. Possessing her. It was both scary and arousing. The realization that she'd do anything this man asked. Anything at all.

While she caressed the heavy weight of her breasts with one hand, she reached beneath her skirt, finding her wet cunt. She ached for him. Needed him. She cried out softly as her fingers brushed her clit, knowing it wouldn't take much to get her to the place where he wanted her.

She glanced towards the hall, but the stacks were empty and she was alone. Just the sound of the air conditioning accompanying her shallow breathing. If anyone came onto the floor, she'd hear the elevator door open. She'd have time to mask what she was doing.

She shook her head, laughing softly. He was going to get her arrested for indecent exposure if she wasn't careful. But that wasn't enough to stop her.

She arched her back, stretching out as she continued circling her clit, her whole body flushed and warm. Somewhere a door slammed shut, making her freeze, her breathing ragged, until she was certain she was alone on the floor.

She slid her finger between her folds, imagining Tristan across campus. She was so wet. So ready. She didn't want to play this game. She wanted him. Here. Now. Didn't care if anyone saw them. She moaned softly. It wouldn't take much to get her off. Not when she was thinking about Tristan's magnificent body spread on top of her, his delicious weight pressing her into the bed while he teased her sex with his glorious cock.

She shuddered, feeling the muscles of her belly clench. God, she wanted to come. Wanted release. Her body fought her mind. He'd know. She didn't know how, but he would. He'd be able to look at her and tell instantly that she'd disobeyed.

She spread her legs wider, granting her fingers better access to explore. Her breasts ached. Heavy with need. Almost painful. Her sex twitched around her fingers as she strummed her clit. She was so close. Her hips bucked up off the chair. Just a little more. She squeezed her eyes shut, her breathing shallow and labored. She bit her lip until the sharp metallic taste of blood brought her back to reality.

No, she'd given him her word. Reluctantly, she pulled her fingers from inside herself, whimpering softly. She needed release. Needed it so badly it hurt. She could smell her arousal. Her labored breathing filled the quiet book lined floor. With trembling fingers, she reached for her phone, her fingers slick with her juices. She knew Tristan was in class but she had no doubt that he'd check his phone the moment he heard it buzz. *Done.* She bit her lip, waiting for his reply.

Good girl. Now put your fingers in your mouth.

A moment later, the phone buzzed again.

When you feel your heart rate return to normal, I want you to do it all over again. Keep this up until I come for you.

Mel shuddered, praying it wouldn't be long.

Mel felt as though her skin was on fire and all it would

take was a light breeze to set her off when she finally heard the door slam shut and Tristan's heavy footsteps approaching. Her skin was flushed, feverish, and she could smell her arousal thick in the air.

She glanced up just as he rounded the corner, catching the smug look on his face as he took her in, feeling his eyes run along her body in slow seduction.

"Took you long enough," she bit out, watching the amusement bloom in his dark eyes. The way he looked at her, it was as though he'd witnessed it all, had witnessed her faithful obedience and wanton desire.

"I almost had to let my students go early," he said gruffly, his voice rough with lust as he closed the distance between them. He pulled her out of her chair, smashing his lips to hers as his hands grabbed a fistful of her hair.

Mel moaned into his mouth. He hoisted her up, and she wrapped her legs tightly around his waist.

"I need you to fuck me, right now," she said, making Tristan chuckle.

"My pleasure," he murmured into her ear, sending a shiver of excitement down to her toes.

A cloud of sex clung to Mel as Tristan propelled her out of the front door of the library. She wondered sleepily if the security guard could tell that they'd just been fucking, but realized with a laugh that she didn't care. Let them know. Let them know she was Tristan's. She couldn't wait to get back to the apartment.

"Colin?" Mel came to abrupt stop as her eyes landed on the last person she expected to see. Colin Dermot. Her ex. "What the hell are you doing here?"

Tristan took a step closer, instinctively shielding her

from the man standing in front of them.

"Carrie said you were here. Can we talk?" Colin glanced at Tristan before looking back at Mel expectantly. "They wouldn't let me in. I tried calling you but your phone went straight to voicemail."

The blissful high she was riding only moments before was eclipsed by the dark circles under his eyes. He wasn't sleeping well, which only made Mel feel worse. She hadn't thought about him once since she ran into Tristan.

Tristan brushed her shoulder, making her start. "Is everything okay?" he asked, keeping his voice low and steady.

Mel straightened, trying to shake off her surprise. "Tristan, this is Colin. My ex," she said, feeling him bristle at her words. Her whole body still hummed from his earlier possession, her thighs sticky with arousal.

"Good to meet you," Tristan bit out without taking his eyes from Mel.

"Do you mind if I have a minute alone with my girlfriend," Colin said finally, his eyes boring into Tristan. Tristan gave her one last look, his dark eyes cold. But beneath that coldness, Mel caught a glimpse of vulnerability that shook her. As if he were begging her to ask him to intervene. When she said nothing, he shrugged indifferently.

"I have to get to class. It was good running into you," he said coldly.

"Who was that?" Colin asked, pulling Mel into a familiar embrace. She pushed him away gently, hoping he wouldn't catch the unmistakable aroma of sex that clung to her skin.

"An old professor," she said finally. "I'm serious,

Colin, what are you doing here?" Even as she said the words, she wished she'd stopped Tristan from walking away. She'd seen the look in his eyes right before he walked off. Hurt. Confusion. Anger. She knew there'd be hell to pay later. If he was even willing to see her.

Mel dismissed the thought. She didn't want to think about the possibility of Tristan walking away. With a resigned shrug, she did her best to smile. She'd deal with Tristan's bruised ego later. "Let's get a cup of coffee."

While Colin ordered, Mel found them a table by the window of the coffee shop on Amsterdam Avenue. She used to come here when she was a student and the familiar setting, even after all that time, comforted her in a way she hadn't expected. She stared out the window, watching people walk past, pulling their jackets close against the gusts of wind. She let out a resigned sigh before turning back to Colin.

He looked the same, albeit slightly shrunken. There were bags under his eyes and she wondered guiltily if he was doing okay. He was wearing jeans and her favorite red flannel shirt, but for some reason, today he looked like a boy. A sweet, kind boy. A boy she'd loved once but didn't love any more. She wished he hadn't come. Didn't know what he was going to say but pretty certain whatever it was would make her feel terrible.

He sat down, pushing her coffee towards her. Black. No sugar. The way she always took her coffee. She took a small sip of the scalding liquid.

"I'm serious, Colin, what are you doing here?" she asked quietly. She didn't want to fight but he needed to understand they were over.

"I miss you," he admitted. "How could you just walk out like that?"

She winced at the hurt in his voice. She didn't want to hurt him. But she needed him to understand.

"I didn't just walk out," she explained patiently. "You slept with someone else. It's over. I got a job for the summer. It's better this way. I don't want to drag this out."

Colin nodded, but it was clear he didn't understand. If he understood, he wouldn't be here.

"I could come with you," he said hopefully. "I'll find a job in Princeton. Mel, we can make this work."

She sighed, struggling to keep her impatience in check. "Colin, that's not going to happen."

"Why not?"

She stared at him, feeling her heart break all over again. "We weren't happy. You slept with a co-worker because we were unhappy. Don't throw away your life so we can do this all over again."

"It would be different this time."

Mel placed her hand over his, giving it a gentle squeeze. "It's over, Colin. You need to go home."

CHAPTER SEVEN

Tristan struggled to make sense of the essay in front of him on decadence in 1920s Paris written by one of the seniors in his class but couldn't concentrate. He'd read a paragraph only to get to the end and realize he had no idea what he'd just read. He rubbed his eyes. Every time he tried to push it from his thoughts, his mind inevitably strayed to Mel and the man he'd left her with. Her ex-boyfriend.

He wanted to punch something just thinking about Mel with him. The thought of him touching her made him sick to his stomach. He wasn't an idiot. He knew perfectly well that they'd had a sexual relationship, but the thought of it was sickening. *His* Mel with another man. He shook his head. Funny, he thought wryly, how suddenly he thought of her as his.

He shouldn't have walked away. He should have stayed, staking his claim. Making it clear to that boy that he'd had his chance and blown it. When she'd said it was over between them, he'd believed her. Hell, he still believed her. Mel wouldn't lie about something like that, he reasoned. Except how well did he really know her? For all he knew, Mel was using him to get back together with her ex. She could be in the back of a taxi with him, heading to the airport to catch the next flight back to Seattle.

He glanced at his phone. He wanted to call her. Wanted to hear her voice. To hear her reassure him that they were fine. But he couldn't bring himself to do it. He tried telling himself he was giving her space to work out whatever was going on between her and her ex, but deep down, he knew that was bullshit. He was a coward. It was that simple. He leaned back and closed his eyes. He should have stayed. He should have made sure Mel was his.

A knock on his door interrupted his thoughts.

"What?" he called out sharply. He wasn't in the mood. There was too much he had to consider without the added distraction of some student stammering excuses as to why they hadn't turned a paper in on time.

Instead, Mel's head appeared in the doorway. "If you're busy, I can come back," she said hastily.

Tristan's heart seized at the sight of her. Her hair was still tousled from their earlier tryst in the library, her lips swollen from his kisses. He shook his head. "No," he said finally, struggling to keep his voice even, "come in. Lock the door behind you."

Mel looked at him nervously before doing as he said, coming to stand in front of his desk with her arms crossed in front of her chest.

She looked beautiful. Light streamed through the opened window, making her hair glow as if on fire.

"Sit down," he said tersely. Watching her stand there

like a nervous student made him uneasy. Hadn't they already broken enough unspoken rules just by being together?

"Do you want to explain what that was all about now or would you like me to give you a good, hard spanking first?" he asked, his voice cold and even. He watched her eyes widen in surprise. God, he wanted to kiss her, but first, he needed her to understand that he had no intention of putting up with exes.

"There's nothing to explain. It's over."

Tristan lifted one eyebrow quizzically but kept his mouth shut. He wanted her to explain. Without his prompting. He wanted to make her squirm for putting him through the torture of the past few hours.

"It's over. He just didn't seem to realize it," she sighed, shifting uncomfortably. "There's nothing going on between us."

"Then why was he here?" The answer was painfully obvious, but he had to ask. Colin wanted her back. Only an idiot would let Mel walk away.

"I don't think he realized I was serious when I left. He told me he'd move to Princeton," she admitted, flinching in anticipation of his response. But Tristan just continued to stare, doing his best to keep his face devoid of emotion.

"What did you say?" he asked softly.

"I told him to go home."

The silence dragged on between them, painful and heavy as they stared across his desk at one another.

Finally, Tristan nodded. "I don't share."

Mel didn't blink. "Neither do I."

Tristan pushed himself out of his chair, coming around the desk and pulling her out of her chair and into a tight embrace. His hands gripped her arms as he smashed his lips down on hers. He needed to know she was his. But first, he wanted to feel his palm connect with the pale skin of her ass. Wanted to witness the signs of his possession clear on her creamy white skin. It might only be for a few days, but Melanie was his. And he wouldn't let her forget it.

Reluctantly, he loosened his grip on her. It was only a question of hours since he'd last buried himself in her tight cunt, fucking her ruthlessly, but it didn't matter. He was hard just thinking about doing it again, feeling her convulse around him as she whimpered in need.

"Take off your dress," he said sharply, walking to the window to lower the blinds. As much as he wanted the world to know she was his, he somehow thought what he had in mind would be best done in private, away from the watching eyes of the university.

When he turned around, Mel stood naked before him. She was stunning. Curvy. Pliant. Her breasts the perfect size and shape for his palms, as though made especially for him. He growled impatiently and walked towards the loveseat against the wall. He briefly considered bending her over his desk and taking her from behind, but the idea of her naked body draped across his lap sounded better. She'd be able to feel his erection digging into her when he slapped her, knowing exactly what she did to him.

He sat down and patted his thigh. Mel nodded, chewing her lip in that way that drove him crazy. He pulled her into one last kiss, letting his hands rake through her hair before releasing her and pushing her down until she was laying across him, her perfect ass in the air. He could smell the delicate scent of her arousal, making his already straining cock twitch in excitement.

"Do you know why I'm doing this?" he asked in a low voice as he rubbed the rounded flesh of her ass beneath his palm.

"Because you're mad at me?" Mel asked uncertainly. Tristan leaned over, pressing a gentle kiss to her shoulder blade.

"I'm not mad at you," he said slowly. "I'm doing this because I want to and because I can. Because it turns me on. I want to see the outline of my palm on your ass and know that you're mine. Only mine. I want to spank you until you forget all about that stupid boy and realize I'm the only man who can satisfy you. I'm going to mark your ass and you're going to thank me. And then I'm going to fuck you," he said roughly, brushing the hair from her shoulder.

Mel's entire body hummed with awareness as moisture pooled between her thighs. She couldn't believe Tristan had her over his lap. She'd never let anyone spank her before. Not that she'd been opposed to the idea. It had simply never arisen.

Tristan's warm hand continued rubbing her flesh, molding her to his hands. He didn't need to mark her skin to claim her. He'd already managed that. But she had no intention of letting him know just how much she'd fallen for him. What had started as childish infatuation had deepened into something else altogether.

Mel tensed as Tristan's fingers danced along her crack, spreading her for him and coming to stop briefly on her puckered entrance. She shivered, knowing instinctively that if he asked for that, she'd give it to him freely. Relief washed over her when his fingers continued their slow exploration, running up and down her slippery folds. Without warning, he sank them into her wet cunt.

His hard-on pressed into her belly, steely and insistent as he stroked her intimately, making her purr.

"God, you're so wet. This excites you, doesn't it?" he whispered into her ear, plunging in and out of her dripping cunt.

"Yes," she moaned, embarrassment flooding her senses. How could she be so turned on by this? All she knew was she didn't want him to stop.

Tristan didn't give her a chance to consider her answer. While one hand continued to fuck her pussy, driving her mad, his palm came down sharply on her ass, making her jump in surprise as she let out a startled cry.

"I don't want to hear a sound coming out of that pretty little mouth of yours unless it's to beg for more," he said in a soft voice. She nodded her head numbly, feeling the tingling heat spread across her glowing skin. The pain quickly dissipated, leaving behind only warmth and awareness. He rubbed her flesh where he'd struck her, soothing her.

"And if you think you're going to come, you had better tell me," he warned, bringing his hand down once more with a loud crack. She bit her lip, stifling a moan.

He alternated, never striking the same place twice, rubbing her tender skin after each blow, soothing her with his touch and his words of encouragement. The feeling was so confusing. She was so turned on, she felt like she might explode, and yet she felt her reaction was wrong. Like she shouldn't be excited. She clenched down on the fingers buried in her cunt, silently begging with her body for a release she knew he wouldn't give her until he was ready. Until he decided she'd had enough. Her ass throbbed, making her acutely aware of her body. She couldn't escape. And each deafening blow made her desperate.

"Please, Tristan," she finally begged after she'd lost count of the number of times he'd smacked her and her body quivered with need.

Tristan chuckled, and she had to bite her lip to stop from cursing him.

"You look stunning wearing my hand print," he whispered gruffly, his voice deep and gravely with barely suppressed need.

He eased her carefully from his lap and onto the seat next to him. Her hair was wild around her face and her lips hung open silently. He unzipped his fly and pulled out his erection, stroking it several times, captivated by Mel's eyes, widening as she watched. He grabbed a condom from his pocket and slid it on expertly.

"Crawl on top of me," he ordered gruffly. "I want you to put me inside you. I want you to fuck me."

Mel straddled him, her perfect breasts just inches from his face as she positioned the head of his cock at her dripping entrance. He palmed her hips, steadying her, holding her in place as he bent down, taking one of her nipples between his teeth, making her hiss.

He wanted to fuck Mel until she couldn't remember anyone before him. Wanted to fuck her until he was all she would ever think about. And he had little doubt that was about to happen.

Tristan lazily stroked Mel's back as she rested her head

against his chest, her breathing finally returned to normal. She fit so perfectly against him.

"Why did you break up?" Tristan asked abruptly. The question had been bothering him since the moment Colin showed up. He needed to know. Needed to know if Mel was the one to walk away or if it was Colin. Because if Colin had walked away, there was a good chance Mel would want him back.

Mel rested her head on his chest as Tristan continued to stroke her back. "He cheated on me," she said softly.

Tristan's fingers stilled. "He what?" He was going to punch that fucker in the face if he ever saw him again. What sort of idiot would cheat when he had a woman like Mel in his bed?

Mel shook her head, smiling up at him sadly, but there was none of the anger or bitterness he'd expected to see. "You're supposed to be pissed when your boyfriend cheats on you, right? Except when he told me, I wasn't even mad. It took a few days for me to realize it, but I didn't care. That was the end. I packed my bags and told him it was over." She gave him a melancholy shrug. "I guess he thought I left him because of it when the truth was, I left because we'd stopped being partners. We lived together but we weren't together. So I booked a ticket and came back to New York."

Tristan watched her sadly. "Now what?"

"I move to Princeton and start my life over, I guess."

"You don't sound thrilled."

"I guess it just seems a little fast. I've wanted this for so long, but now that it's happening, it doesn't feel real. I'm excited to start classes, but what if I'm not cut out for it? What if I can't find a job when I graduate? Or I hate

Princeton?"

Tristan's jaw clenched. "That's the stupidest thing I've ever heard come out of that beautiful mouth of yours," he said fiercely. "They picked you out of hundreds of other applicants because you deserve this. Because they believe in you. I believe in you. Don't sell yourself short. You're way too smart to think that way." She looked away in embarrassment which only pissed him off more. "I'm serious, Mel."

She nodded into his chest, feeling his arm tighten around her, holding her against him. "I know. That doesn't mean it's any less scary, though."

He kissed her forehead reassuringly. "We should probably go. Someone in the office might start to worry."

Mel laughed and Tristan helped her to her feet. She looked soft and pliant, satisfaction making her whole body relaxed. He liked seeing her like this. Carefree. Easy.

"Let me take you out to dinner tonight. You're leaving in two days."

Mel beamed up at him. "I'd love that."

They were seated at a small restaurant on Broadway, not far from Tristan's apartment.

"It's only April. Why are you going up to school so early?"

Mel took a measured sip of her wine. "I wasn't supposed to go until July but when everything with Colin happened, I made a few calls. Mary Taylor was looking for a research assistant for the summer and she hired me."

Tristan felt his heart sink, hating himself for his selfish reaction. Mary Taylor was a big deal. She'd worked in the Comparative Literature Department at Princeton since the seventies, routinely publishing papers and attending conferences. He'd met her a number of times over the years and was always struck by her shrewd intellect and unexpected humor. Working with her would be an amazing experience for Mel.

"That's great," he said, trying to mask his disappointment. Had he really hoped she'd stay in New York longer? "When do you start?"

"As soon as the semester ends. This gives me a little time to find an apartment and settle in."

He nodded. Obviously, that made perfect sense. So why did it make he feel terrible? He'd always enjoyed relationships with women to have a definite end point. It stopped things from getting messy. At least most of the time. Still, he couldn't help but feel disappointed. He wanted more time. A taste wasn't enough. He wanted more.

"I'm sure you won't have any trouble there," he said at last. Mel watched him over the rim of her glass, her lips parted as though she wanted to say something.

"Yeah, I'm sure it will be fine."

For a brief instant, he considered offering her a position as his research assistant. The university was always pestering him about such things, but he'd always declined, saying he preferred working alone. Which was true. But maybe he just hadn't found the right research assistant.

Tristan clenched his fists under the table. No, that was a terrible idea. For both of them. Working with Mary Taylor would be a boon for Mel and taking that away from her just so he could fuck her for a few more months wasn't fair.

"Are you ready to go?" he asked, suddenly impatient to

get Mel back to his apartment. If they only had 48 hours left, he wanted them to count. His lips curled into a seductive smile. "I thought we'd have dessert at home."

Mel's lips parted in surprise before she threw back her head, her musical laughter attracting the attention of the other diners. She crumpled her napkin and threw it down on the table. "Ready."

He wondered if she realized she was the only dessert he had planned.

CHAPTER EIGHT

The apartment was bathed in shadows, the light streaming in from outside illuminating the shapes of the furniture. Tristan gripped her arms, spinning her around to face him. Her eyes sparkled in the darkness.

"I'm going to tie you up and fuck you hard," he said before crushing his lips to hers, feeling her soften in his arms.

"Don't you ever get tired?" She laughed loudly.

"How could I possibly get tired of having my way with you?" he asked, but what he was really thinking was, how could he tell her he'd never been like this before? That normally he'd have been more than satisfied with just one of their trysts of the day? Instead, he reached beneath her skirt, finding her wet cunt warm and waiting. "Especially when you're always ready."

She sagged into him as he slide two fingers into her, spreading her. "I'm not always ready," she tried to protest but her body told him otherwise.

He shook his head. "You show the world your prim

façade, but deep down, you know you need this. Need to be taken. Fucked. You look like a nice girl who wants a man to make love to her, but you're not. You're a woman who needs a man who will fuck you mercilessly."

He trailed kisses down her neck, loving the way she trembled in his arms.

"Tristan," she said, her voice shaking slightly, "I think maybe we should go to the bedroom now."

He brought his fingers to his lips, smiling as he sucked them into his mouth. "I think I'm going to enjoy dessert very much tonight," he said wickedly. "I want you naked on the bed when I come in," he said, swatting her playfully on the ass.

The hair on Mel's head prickled in anticipation as she waited, naked, on the bed for Tristan. She was so turned on, so ready for him. She sighed.

When Tristan finally appeared in the doorway, she sucked in a deep breath, letting her eyes trail over him languidly. He was perfect. His body strong and dominant. He gave her a wicked smile that she could feel down to her core, filling her with excitement. In his hand was a long length of black satin rope. She licked her lips nervously. Whatever Tristan had planned for tonight, it would be an unforgettable experience.

"Get on your knees and turn around," he said forcefully as he strode towards her. She nodded, following his command. She felt the bed dip as he kneeled behind her and he lifted her hair from her neck, placing a kiss to the sensitive skin at the base of her neck, making her shiver. His touch was electric. She could feel it all the way to her cunt. Electric and erotic and inescapable. He trailed kisses across her shoulder blades, lavishing attention on her skin.

He took her hands in his, bringing them together behind her back and looping the rope around her wrists until they were tightly bound together. She attempted to move them, only to hear him chuckle.

"You aren't getting away that easily," he said with a chuckle. "Turn around."

Mel struggled to face him, feeling the awkwardness of having her hands bound behind her. She looked up at him expectantly and he smiled at her reassuringly, running a finger down her check and brushing it across her full mouth. He kissed her tenderly, his tongue slipping between her lips in an erotic dance. Her nipples hardened painfully as her body begged for release.

He stepped back and she could feel his admiring gaze on her skin. He grabbed another piece of black satin, making Mel's heart tighten in anticipation. He parted her legs until she was spread wide for him, her breasts forced forward as her back arched, her wet cunt displayed lewdly. He ran a finger along her seam, making her shudder as she bit her lip, stifling a moan.

With a tender yet forceful hand, he wound the satin between her upper thigh and her ankle, binding her leg in position before doing the same to her other leg. In this position, she could barely move and the thought sent a wave of excitement through her.

"Tristan?" she asked nervously and he just looked up at her, his velvety eyes dark with lust as he drank her in. No one had ever looked at her like that. Like she was perfect. Fragile. Precious. Like he couldn't get enough.

"Are you okay?" he asked.

She nodded, biting her lip.

"Good." With that, he wound the final piece of black satin across her eyes, cutting off her sight. "Now," he said, chuckling, "I think it's time for dessert."

Mel awoke crushed beneath Tristan's heavy arm. She eased his arm off of her, careful not to wake him and stared up at the ceiling. In less than 36 hours, she was leaving. Her bags were packed. Everything left in Seattle would be shipped once she found somewhere to live. She listened to Tristan's heavy, even breaths. He was so peaceful when he slept. So still. She wanted to reach out and touch him but she was afraid she'd wake him and she knew he had an early class in the morning.

She was going to miss him, she realized sadly, feeling her eyes burn. Crazy, after only five days, but it was true. She hadn't even left yet and she could already feel the sadness welling up inside of her, threatening to make her cry. She was going to miss him and there was nothing she could do about it.

She rolled onto her side, pressing her lips to his muscular back. She inhaled the sharp, masculine scent of him that was already so familiar, so comforting. She didn't want to miss him. It would be a hard enough adjustment without having to deal with this. Hell, if she'd known it was going to be this hard, that she'd fall for him this quickly, maybe she wouldn't have accepted his offer to take her out for a drink.

She smiled to herself sadly, knowing she was only deluding herself. No matter how hard it was going to be to leave him behind, she wouldn't give this time up for anything. It wouldn't be pleasant, but she'd survive.

But 36 hours was so little time. She bit her lip in frustration. She could call Mary Taylor and tell her something had come up. There were three weeks until the end of term. That would be plenty of time to find a suitable replacement.

But opportunities like this didn't come along every day. She sighed, wishing there were some easy answer. Had Tristan expressed any interest in having her stay, she'd probably have already called Mary Taylor. But he'd been remarkably tight-lipped on the subject. She saw the way he looked at her when he thought she wasn't paying attention. Unless she was totally mistaken, there was more there than simple lust, though there was certainly a lot of that as well.

How many times had he taken her in the last few days? How many earth-shattering orgasms had he given her? Being with him was like a dream she didn't want to wake up from. How do you just walk away from something like that?

She wanted to ask his advice. Wanted to know what he was thinking. She wished they could have a real conversation about this, about what was happening and what would happen. Only that was never going to happen. She knew what he'd say. He'd tell her not to be an idiot. He'd tell her to go to Princeton, to work for Mary Taylor. Because that was the right thing to do. Even if it hurt. Even if it meant walking away from him. Never in a million years would he ask her to stay. She rolled onto her back and stared at the ceiling, listening to the oceanic sounds of his breath, wishing there were some other way. Because the idea of getting on that train and leaving him sounded horrible.

CHAPTER NINE

Tristan considered cancelling his ten a.m. lecture to stay in bed with Mel. His students would be thrilled. They had a paper due and it would give them some much needed extra time. Not that he was thinking about his students. No, he was thinking about Mel's warm little body curled at his side in sleep. She looked so peaceful, her body soft and warm and he realized this was where he wanted to be. Fuck class. Fuck teaching. He wanted to be right here, with Mel in his arms.

He eased her legs apart and slowly slid his hard cock into her lovely cunt, quietly fucking her with a gentleness that surprised him. He'd taken her roughly before. He'd tied her up and fucked her publicly. This morning, he wanted only to savor the feel of her in his arms. Wanted to gently coax an orgasm from her still sleeping body. More than anything, he wanted to make love to her, he realized almost in disgust.

"You're going to get fired if you keep this up," Mel

said, giving him a playful shove when he told her he was thinking of canceling his class. "I'll be here when you get back."

Women didn't usually push Tristan out of bed. Especially *his* bed. Normally he was happy to see them go in the morning, if they even spent the night. He wasn't used to spending time with a woman and liking it. He'd spent his entire life wrapped up in school and his career. First it was college. Then his doctorate. Then teaching and all the university drama.

Maybe it was the knowledge that she was leaving in the morning that allowed him to live presently. To enjoy each moment. Tomorrow she'd get the train at Penn Station and he'd likely never see her again.

The thought made his head ache. He didn't like the idea of her leaving in the first place. The idea that he might never see her again? He groaned.

He couldn't understand what was happening. What any of this meant. He liked her. Liked spending time with her. Liked knowing she'd be at his apartment when he got home at the end of his day.

The fact that she was leaving only highlighted his desire to spend time with her now. She'd been clear she didn't expect anything from him. She'd said as much when they were laying on the couch in his office, recovering from one of the most exquisite sexual experiences of his life. Just thinking about it made him hard.

She was leaving. And he couldn't ask her to stay. It was fucking Princeton! How he would have reacted if someone had been stupid enough to suggest he not go to Harvard for his PhD? He'd have been furious. And Mel would have every right to be equally livid if he asked her to give up her dream on the promise of what? An affair? The idea was ludicrous.

He knew how hard she'd worked for this and there was no fucking way he could ask her to sacrifice that just because he didn't like the idea of giving her up. He was a selfish prick in a lot of ways, but not about this. No, this he understood perfectly.

He slammed his fist down on his desk, cursing loudly. He was stuck here for another thirty minutes and then he was heading straight back to his apartment. The only stop he'd make was to pick up something for them to eat. He wanted to enjoy every moment they had left together. Because the more he thought about it, the less he liked the idea of letting her go.

Tristan was packing up his things, getting ready to head home, when a knock on the door made him look up. "What?" he called out impatiently.

Doctor Thomas Reeves, the head of the English Department, filled the doorway. Tristan groaned to himself. Whatever this was, it would take a while. Thomas Reeves had the irritating habit of droning on, particularly when he was least wanted.

"What can I do for you?" Tristan asked, feeling a pang of anxiety as Thomas Reeves took a seat in front of his desk.

It was a quarter to four by the time Thomas Reeves finally left his office. He'd wasted enough time. If Mel was hungry, they could order in. Or go out somewhere. He'd happily take her out to a very late lunch, though the idea of sharing her with a restaurant full of people didn't exactly appeal to him.

What the hell was wrong with him? Never in his life had he been this obsessed by a woman. This irrationally possessive. Sure, he was always a possessive man. The type of man unwilling to share what was his. But this went beyond that, he realized, impatiently tapping his foot as the elevator crawled up to the twelfth floor.

He should be getting a head start on grading the stack of papers tucked in his briefcase, but there was no way he was getting to work until Mel left. There wasn't any point in trying. He was too distracted to concentrate properly and it would likely take twice as long to get even half as much done as normal.

He was obsessed. That was the only word he could think of. This was an obsession and perhaps the sooner she left, the better. She'd leave and he'd finally be able to think properly. He'd almost had a heart attack when Thomas Reeves walked into his office wanting to talk to him. Not because he'd done anything wrong. While the university would likely be less than thrilled to find out one of their tenured professors was busy fucking a woman all over campus, an ex-student no less, there really wasn't much they could do to stop him. In a moment of weakness, he'd even asked Thomas about hiring a summer research assistant and watched Thomas' face light up in excitement.

Too bad the only research assistant he'd ever consider already had a better offer two hours south of the city.

He unlocked the door, dropping his briefcase to the ground and came to an abrupt halt. He closed his eyes, letting the delicious smell of roasted garlic wash over him.

"Mel?" he called out in surprise. Mel popped her head

out of the kitchen and there was a smudge of flour on her cheek that made her look adorable.

"What in God's name are you doing?"

"Cooking, what do you think?"

He looked around his usually spotless kitchen in amazement. There were bowls and plates everywhere. The sink was filled with dishes and she'd somehow managed to get flour on every possible surface. But what distressed Tristan most was that he actually liked seeing her there, in his kitchen, surrounded by disorder. For the first time since he'd moved in, his apartment felt suddenly like a home.

"I realize it's a little late for lunch and way too early for dinner," she apologized with a shrug. "Anyway, it's just a little thank you for letting me stay here."

He looked at her in wonder. Where else would he have let her stay? Would it have really made sense for her to go between his bed and the couch in her friend's apartment half-way across the city?

"You didn't have to…"

She looked at him sharply. "I wanted to so try not to ruin it."

Everything was going terribly wrong. He wasn't supposed to enjoy having her here. She wasn't supposed to look so fucking adorable cooking. Since when did adorable even appeal to him? He was supposed to be relieved that she was leaving in the morning. Relieved that he'd have his space back to himself, that he'd finally be able to concentrate on something other than his dick, which only seemed to be satisfied when buried deep inside her perfect fucking cunt.

He groaned. He was fucked.

Mel appeared in the living room carrying a tray laden with dishes. Whatever she'd made, it smelled delicious. "Where should I put this?"

Tristan stared at her, then finally shook his head and crossed the room, taking the tray from her. "I've got it," he said, leading the way to the dining table that he so rarely used. He never had guests and didn't see the point of setting the table when he was eating alone, but from the looks of it, Mel had made enough food that they'd need the damned thing, after all.

"I went a little overboard," she said, laughing and wiping her hands on her thighs.

He unloaded the steaming plates on the table. "What is it?"

"Moroccan chicken with couscous," she said with a self-conscious shrug.

Tristan pulled her towards him and gave her a sweet kiss. She tasted amazing. Tart, like lemons. And just a little sweet. He leaned back and brushed the flour from her face with his thumb.

"You really didn't have to do all this." He would have been perfectly content eating Chinese takeout straight from the containers as long as she was there.

"Come on, I wanted to wow you with my culinary prowess. Plus, I don't really like sitting around with nothing to do."

Tristan stared at her, worrying briefly that this dinner might not just be a dinner, but something more. That she might be trying to get something from him. But the honesty and simplicity in Mel's expression made him brush away his doubts. Mel wouldn't try to manipulate him, especially not with food. Especially after he'd foolishly made it clear that he expected this to end the moment she left.

"I'll get the wine," he said, relieved to have something to do.

Tristan found a bottle of white wine in the fridge and they sat down to dinner. She looked stunning, as always, her hair wild around her shoulders and he was dying to twine his hands in it, to lose himself in its softness.

The food was just as amazing as it smelled and when Tristan finally pushed back his seat, full and warm and content, Mel shot out of her chair and darted to the kitchen.

"I made an apple cake!" she screamed over her shoulder. He groaned. He couldn't imagine putting another bite of food in his body, but if Mel baked a cake, he damn well knew he'd eat it.

She returned moments later carrying what could only be generously described as a very rustic looking cake.

"Are you sure that's fit to eat?" he asked, eyeing the cake suspiciously. It had lumps. Cakes were certainly not meant to have lumps.

"Oh come on. It's a little funny looking but I promise it's delicious. Scout's honor and all that."

He watched her sadly as she served him a slice. When she put the knife down, he looped his arm around her waist, dragging her onto his lap and nuzzling her warm, fragrant neck. He kissed her, feeling her melt into his arms. He didn't want her to go. He just couldn't ask her to stay.

He ran his hands over her thighs, bunching her dress around her waist. He wanted to lose himself in her body. Lose himself in sensation. Because when he was buried deep inside Mel, he couldn't think about the future.

Mel was tucked comfortably under his arm, her head resting on his chest as he stroked her back, and Tristan found himself wanting to ask her what she was thinking. She was so silent and still that at first he thought she'd dozed off, but then he'd felt her nuzzle even closer and realized she was still awake.

Instead, he asked what time her train left in the morning. He felt her stiffen slightly before she propped herself up on her elbow, staring up at him, her green eyes wide. "Noon," she said, making his heart pound faster.

Twelve hours. Just twelve hours. He knew they both needed to get some sleep, but sleep seemed like a cruel waste of their final hours together.

"Do you know what your schedule is with Mary Taylor yet?"

He let his hand roam down her back, feeling the gentle curve of her ass beneath his palm, cupping her to him. Somehow, feeling her naked skin made this conversation easier to tolerate.

Mel shook her head. "No, she said the hours would depend on how her book is coming along."

"It'll be a great experience." He let his head drop back on the pillow. "You should get some sleep," he said finally, rolling over and hitting the light switch, plunging the room into darkness. He felt Mel snuggle closer, her body warm and comforting and familiar. He knew he could ask her to stay. Knew he could suggest she work for him. Except that would be so fucking wrong.

He wanted to groan. Instead, he rolled onto his side away from Mel. They'd deal with tomorrow when it came.

CHAPTER TEN

Mel woke up feeling groggy, her head aching slightly. She hadn't slept well. After Tristan abruptly told her to get some sleep, she'd lain awake, trying not to disturb him as she replayed his words.

Her mind raced with familiar anxiety she hadn't experienced recently. Did he want her to leave? Was he looking forward to having his apartment and his life back? The thought filled her with anguish. At times, it felt as if he couldn't get enough of her. The way he rushed back from campus, his reluctance to leave the apartment. But then he'd turned out the light and rolled onto his side, his body language making the distance between them clear.

When she finally opened her eyes, she was alone in bed. She could hear the shower running in the other room and she couldn't help but feel a stab of disappointment.

She'd wanted to wake up next to him one last time.

Yesterday, she would have bolted from bed and joined him in the shower, excited at the thought of his soap slick body, but today, she knew that wasn't what he wanted.

She'd thought she'd at least have until she left for the train, but already, he was putting distance between them. He was dismissing her. Discarding her. And it hurt. More than she wanted to admit.

How did you really expect this to go, she admonished herself, slipping from the bed and padding over to her suitcase. Did you really expect him to beg you to stay? Tristan was too proud of a man to beg. Even if he wanted her to stay.

She bit her lip and dug through her bag for the outfit she planned on wearing on the train. Super soft leggings and a chambray shirt. Comfort clothing she rarely wore out of the house, but she needed something to make her feel better when the truth was, she could feel her heart breaking in her chest.

When Tristan finally emerged from the shower, a towel wrapped loosely around his waist, she was dressed and sitting on the bed. He cocked his head, eyeing her silently before going to his dresser.

"Sorry if I woke you," he said without turning. She watched his steady movements as he pulled on a pair of jeans and a t-shirt. He ran the towel through his hair before throwing it onto the bed.

"Do you want to get breakfast?" He checked his watch. "I have to be on campus in an hour but there should be time to grab a coffee."

Mel's heart sank. What had she really been expecting? That he'd order her out of her clothes before throwing her down on the bed and fucking her one last time? Yesterday, that's exactly what he would have done. But this morning, he was all business. Gone was the passionate man she'd come to love in the past few days.

"Coffee sounds great," she answered hollowly. Her stomach felt like it was tied in knots and she didn't think she'd be able to choke down anything but coffee.

For a long moment, he just looked at her, unspeaking, his jaw tense. She wanted to say something to bridge the gap widening between them, but instead she just watched him sadly.

Finally, he nodded. "You can come back for your bags."

They sat across from each other at a bagel shop on Broadway. When Mel had only ordered a large black coffee, he'd looked at her sharply and insisted she have a bagel as well. It was a long train ride and the least he could do was buy her breakfast. Mel looked at him blankly and shrugged like she couldn't care less about food. He knew the feeling. His stomach was too unsteady for food.

He wanted to say something. The silence between them was torture. They'd never been like this. He ran his hand through his damp hair, knowing he could still ask her to stay. The way she was staring blankly at her untouched bagel, it was obvious he was the one who'd have to speak. He regretted getting out of bed this morning to shower but he hadn't been able to sleep. His mind had kept racing. Normally, he'd have gone for a run but he didn't want Mel to wake up alone in the apartment. In the end, it hadn't mattered. She was dressed, one foot practically out the door.

He wished he could ask her to stay. The university would pay her. She could stay with him. She wouldn't have to worry about rent. Hell, she'd be able to save some money before classes started in the fall. And he wouldn't have to give her up.

But that's what he'd asked her for. Five days. Just five days and then they'd go their separate ways. He sighed, staring out the window as the passersby. It was a sunny morning, the first real day that felt like spring, and students wore t-shirts and shorts, smiling as they walked down Broadway, the light hitting their young faces.

"Mel," he started, causing her to glance up from the napkin she was playing with. The weary hope in her eyes made his courage fail him. It was better this way, he reminded himself. He couldn't give her what she deserved. He was being the bigger man in letting her go. And sometimes being the bigger man felt like shit. Even if it was the right thing to do.

"What?"

"Nothing." He glanced at his watch. "I can take you to Penn Station if you want," he said at last.

"I thought you had a meeting."

He shrugged. "It can wait. I'd feel better knowing you made your train."

He was an asshole but that was the best he could offer her. He watched her crumple into her chair and he wanted to reach over and take her hand. Wanted to tell her this wasn't the end but the beginning. The beginning of what, he still didn't know. Instead, he stared at his coffee.

Mel picked up her suitcase but Tristan took it from her gently. She barely recognized this man. He wasn't the passionate man she'd just spent five of the most amazing days of her life with. He was acting like nothing had happened, his demeanor as coldly polite as it had been when she was his student. She wanted to poke a finger at his chest and yell at him. How could he just push her out of his life like that? How could he act like it hadn't meant anything?

Mel stopped at the door and turned to look at him. "You know," she said cautiously, "Princeton is only a two hour train ride from here."

She watched his whole body tense as he gazed down at her, his eyes dark and unreadable.

"I know where Princeton is," he said stiffly. Mel couldn't help but reach out and place her hand on his arm, wanting to feel him alive beneath her fingers. Just one last time before she left.

If she didn't try, she knew she'd never forgive herself. His rejection would sting, but at least she'd have tried. At least she'd know for certain. That she hadn't let her pride keep her from asking for the one thing she really wanted.

"I could visit," she said softly.

He watched her cautiously. "Do you want to visit?" he asked slowly, his voice carefully guarded.

"I don't want this to end. I know I agreed to five days, but right now, that seems like total lunacy to me. If I'm wrong, tell me, and I'll never mention this again. I don't know what any of this means, but I don't want to lose you, either."

For one strained moment, Mel watched him, her heart beating frantically in her chest as she steeled herself against the emotional blow to come. But when Tristan's lips curled into a relieved smile, she exhaled the breath she hadn't even realized she was holding.

"You can catch the later train," he said, letting her bag drop to the floor with a thud. "Right now, I want you naked in my bed in thirty seconds or the spanking I give you will make that two hour train ride seem like an eternity."

Mel grinned. "Promise?"

PART TWO

CHAPTER ONE

Tristan stared impatiently at the clock, wondering how on earth it was only Wednesday. It felt like the week would never end.

"Professor Everett?"

Tristan glanced at the student shifting restlessly in the chair in front of him. The nervous way he avoided Tristan's eyes made him wonder just how long he'd been staring at the clock. He cleared his throat. "Sorry, what were you saying?"

"Are you okay? I can come back later if this isn't a good time."

Tristan wanted to laugh. Was he okay? No, he was obviously not okay. Since when did Tristan Everett space out in the middle of office hours? Since when did he have trouble concentrating on anything? He was a complete fucking mess and it was all Melanie Potter's fault.

"I'm fine," Tristan answered tersely. He had zero interest in discussing his personal problems with a student. Which was ironic, given the circumstances.

Tristan sighed. He was having a hard time keeping it together. He was accustomed to commanding respect from his students with little more than a sharp look, but he found his control slipping and he wasn't the least bit surprised that his students had started slacking off as a result. The paper in front of him was a complete disaster, but how could he blame them? They were simply following his example.

Since running into Mel in the library, everything had changed. She'd gotten under his skin and he wasn't prepared for it. He'd assumed their affair would last the five days she was in New York, and while he hadn't wanted to let her go, that's exactly what he'd been prepared to do. It was Mel who insisted that they continue seeing each other, even though she was now in Princeton and he was still in New York.

It had seemed simple enough at the time. They'd continue sleeping together when their busy schedules allowed. The problem was, Tristan found himself counting down the minutes until he could see her again.

It was killing him. If it weren't so distressing, Tristan would have laughed. It took all of Tristan's willpower to drag his attention back to the marked up term paper on the desk in front of him. He couldn't believe a woman was having this affect on him.

"I'm sorry, let's get back to your paper. Do you have any other questions? I know you were struggling with the introduction."

But Melanie wasn't just any woman. There was something about her. Something Tristan had never been able to put his finger on. He'd seen it when she was his student, which was why he'd always kept his distance, taking care never to be alone with her. The few times she'd come to office hours had been pure torture. Sitting alone in a room with that irresistible woman, willing himself not to stare. Just being in the same room as Mel was enough to make him hard.

Yes, Mel was definitely gorgeous, but it was more than her uncommon beauty. It was something about her, something about the woman that she was, that drew him in, trivializing everything else in the process. When she was his student, he'd done everything to ignore that attraction, making sure to keep their relationship as professional as possible.

But everything had changed. She wasn't his student any longer. She was a grown woman, about to start graduate school. And she was his.

All he had to do was get through the next two days. Then Mel was coming to the city for the weekend. For now, he had to focus. Even if that seemed absolutely impossible.

Sometimes she felt like a dream. Too good to be true after all the time he'd spent imagining what it would be like to touch her, to taste her, to feel her supple body beneath his. But she was real. God, she was real. And his dick throbbed just thinking about the way she looked up at him with those large green eyes, wide and innocent. But she was anything but innocent as she begged for his touch.

"Professor Everett?"

Tristan dug his nails into his palms, trying to clear his mind. This was getting absolutely fucking ridiculous. "Is there anything else?"

The student shook his head, gathering his things off Tristan's desk and scurrying out of the office. Tristan let out a sigh of relief once the office door slammed shut.

He grabbed his phone off his desk. Maybe it made him a selfish asshole, but he wanted to know she was suffering just as much as he was.

Mel glanced at the pile of books she needed to annotate before the weekend and sighed wearily. No matter how much she loved working as Professor Taylor's research assistant, there were moments when she wished she'd stayed in New York. Not that she'd had a reason to stay, except Tristan. But Tristan was reason enough.

He was like a fucking drug and she couldn't wait for her next fix. The fact that she never knew when it would come kept her perpetually on edge.

Mel jumped, startled by the sound of her phone. Tristan's name flashed on the screen and she shot out of her chair, apologizing to Professor Taylor as she stepped into the hall.

"Hey," she whispered, closing the door softly behind her. "Is everything okay?"

"What are you doing?" Tristan asked at last in that sexy voice of his that made Mel's whole body burn with anticipation.

"I'm at work."

"What time do you get off?"

"Soon, why?"

"There's something I want you to do."

Mel noted the rough edge to his voice and she felt a wave of desire flow through her body. "Okay…"

"Do you have a pen?"

Mel hurried through the shopping mall, Tristan's words

still ringing in her ears. *Take yourself shopping. Buy yourself something that makes you feel sexy.*

When she asked what he wanted her to buy, he told her it didn't matter. All he wanted was for her to find something that made her feel beautiful. Something that made her feel sexy. *I want you thinking about me even when I'm not there. I want you to remember I'm always there with you.* Then he'd read off his credit card number and hung up before Mel could say another word.

He left her breathless and on edge. He knew there was no way she'd be able to get him out of her mind now. Mel stepped into a high-end lingerie store, noting the racks of brightly colored lace and satin.

Just running her fingers along the delicate lingerie, feeling the sumptuous fabric against her skin, she felt decadent, sensual, and she couldn't help but smile. She knew this was Tristan's intention. He wanted her brimming with awareness, unable to escape him. Tristan wasn't content knowing that he had her body. He wanted her mind as well.

She couldn't believe he still didn't realize she'd been his from the start.

Mel looked around, momentarily overwhelmed by the selection of gorgeous lingerie. Tristan once told her that he loved the way she let the world think she was prim and proper when the truth was, when she was with him, she was anything but. He said he loved that he was the only person who ever saw that side of her. But tonight, Mel wanted to find something to show him just how sexy she could be.

"Can I help you?"

Mel jumped, then laughed, embarrassed at being caught

off guard. Turning around, she found a tall woman smiling at her expectantly and it took Mel a moment to realize that she worked there. There was something about the woman standing in front of her, her small upturned nose and freckled cheeks, that piqued Mel's interest and Mel had to try not to stare.

Mel shook her head.

"My boyfriend is coming into town and I want to get something special." It felt strange referring to Tristan as her boyfriend, but how else could she describe him? Her lover? The man who drove her crazy with need? Mel felt her face turn red. Boyfriend was definitely safer.

"Great," the woman said, brushing her bangs out of her eyes and Mel caught a glimpse of a star-shaped tattoo on her inner wrist. There was something so unexpectedly sensual about that innocent gesture and that tiny black tattoo..."Let's get you a fitting room and I can take your measurements and we can go from there."

Mel shook off her confusion and trailed behind the woman towards the fitting rooms at the back of the store, watching the gentle sway of her hips as she moved. Mel had never found herself attracted to women before, but there was something so alluring about the way she moved. Her almost dancer's poise and Mel had to bite her lip, trying to stop herself from imagining what she would look like naked.

What was it about Tristan that had her thinking about sex constantly?

Mel slipped into the ornately decorated fitting room, taking in the cream-colored wallpaper and intricate toile furnishings.

"My name's Sam. Why don't you get undressed and I'll

be back in a moment."

Mel pulled her dress over her head, feeling a wave of nervous energy. It wasn't fair that she was the one always suffering, always itching for more when there was no relief in sight and Tristan remained perfectly poised. Like he was untouchable. Like he was immune to what was going on between them.

She grabbed her phone. Two could play at this game.

Are you happy? I'm horny and naked and there's a very attractive woman about to fit me for a bra.

She slipped her phone into her purse with a self-satisfied smile. That would give Tristan something to think about.

"All ready?"

Before Mel could even open her mouth, Sam popped her head through the curtain. "How long have you been with your boyfriend?" she asked, motioning for Mel to stand in front of the mirror. Suddenly the spacious fitting room felt too small and Mel stared at their reflection in the mirror. Sam's delicate fingers gently wrapped the tape measure around her breasts and Mel held her breath.

"A few months," Mel breathed out, noticing with mounting embarrassment that her nipples were hard and visible through her bra. She shifted restlessly. She couldn't believe she was turned on right now.

"What's he like?"

Mel snorted. "One of a kind."

The woman laughed. "Well, I'm sure we'll find something perfect to knock his socks off. I'll be right back with some things for you to try on."

Mel blushed as she reread Tristan's text message. *I see*

you've been keeping secrets from me. You never said you were attracted to girls.

Mel realized too late that she was playing a game she had no hope of winning. Tristan was better at this. He always would be.

I'm not, usually.

What's different about her?

Mel squeezed her eyes shut, trying to pinpoint what had caught her attention the second she saw Sam, but it was useless. There was just something about Sam. Something Mel couldn't identify. *I don't know.*

Don't be coy. I want to know what kind of woman turns you on.

She could hear the gentle reproach in his voice and she tried not to think as she responded. *There's just something sexual about her. About the way she looked at me. She's beautiful, but it's more than that.*

Mel held her breath as she stared at her phone, waiting for Tristan's response. She could feel her pulse racing.

Describe her.

Mel swallowed hard, her mouth suddenly dry. *She has a little tattoo on her wrist. Seeing it made me think there might be more to her than meets the eye. She's beautiful, but maybe she's also a little wild.* Mel bit her lip before adding. *I've always wondered what it would be like to go down on a woman.*

Mel squeezed her eyes shut in embarrassment after hitting send. She couldn't believe she'd actually just written that. But Tristan had a way of getting her to do things she never would have considered before.

God, I can't imagine anything more incredible than watching a beautiful woman lick your pussy until you came apart.

Mel's lips parted in astonishment. When her phone vibrated again, Mel felt a familiar pulse start between her legs and her heart pounded in her chest. *Ask for her number.*

"Can I come in?"

Mel blushed, scrambling to hide her phone. She could practically smell her arousal in the air.

"I have a few things for you to try, but I really think this is going to be the best," Sam said, holding up a cherry red bustier that reminded Mel of 1950s pin-ups. "The color will look fantastic with your skin."

Before she had a chance to think, Mel took a deep breath and reached back, unclasping her bra and letting it slide down her arms until she was standing in front of Sam in nothing but her panties. She couldn't believe she was doing this, and yet, she knew it was exactly what Tristan would want.

When she glanced at her reflection in the mirror, she saw how hard her nipples were and she squeezed her eyes shut, trying to imagine what it would be like with Tristan and another woman. Somehow, Tristan made anything and everything possible. It terrified her, but God, did it make her wet.

Tristan paced his living room, waiting to hear back from Mel. He shouldn't have asked her to do that. They'd never discussed the possibility of sleeping with other people, together or apart, and he worried he might have pushed her too far. Until tonight, Mel had never expressed any interest in women and her comment had caught him off guard. Now, though, he wondered if he should have let it slide. He hadn't been thinking clearly. He wasn't kidding when he said he couldn't imagine anything more incredible than watching another woman pleasure Mel.

Tristan cursed and rearranged himself in his pants,

wishing he could have seen the look on Mel's face. The surprise. The uncertainty. He loved seeing her like that. When she didn't know if she'd be able to do what he asked. Watching the way her mind fought against her body, against her own arousal.

His sole intention had been to drive Mel wild, to have her burning to see him. Instead, he was the one who felt like the weekend couldn't come fast enough.

Tristan drained his glass of wine. He needed to hear from her. Needed to know that she hadn't panicked. He glanced at the clock. It had been a half hour. That was more than enough time. He grabbed his phone and texted her, asking if she'd done what he'd asked. He held his breath as he waited, tapping his foot against the hardwood floor. He didn't like being kept waiting.

Yes.

Tristan groaned. God, he wanted to fuck her so bad it hurt.

Are you wet?

Tristan freed himself from the tight confines of his pants, unable to resist the urge to pleasure himself as he waited for Mel's response. And when it came, he let out of a sigh of relief.

Yes. I wish you were here to fuck me.

His lips curled into a satisfied smile. God, he loved knowing Mel was just as turned on as he was, that she needed this just as much as he did.

Soon. Now get your ass home. I want you to fuck yourself until you come, imagining that woman between your legs, licking your pussy. I want you to imagine I'm there, watching you with her.

CHAPTER TWO

Mel cursed when she realized that it was already six and she wasn't anywhere near finished with all the reading she needed to do for Monday. No matter how much she'd been looking forward to this weekend, she knew she'd have to cancel on Tristan. There was no way she'd be able to go the city and expect to get anything done while she was there.

Because when she was with Tristan, the absolute last thing on her mind was work. Their weekend would have to wait. It sucked, but she couldn't let Professor Taylor down. Not when working with her was such a big deal. Professor Taylor was the type of person who could open doors for her and she wasn't about to waste the opportunity on a fuck.

Not that Tristan was just a fuck. She could tell herself it was just sex as much as she wanted, but she missed him. And it wasn't just his body that she missed. She missed the beautiful, intelligent, domineering man she'd fallen for when she was his student.

Mel hated that she missed him. Hated that she couldn't stop thinking about him. No matter how many times she told herself it was just sex – mind-blowing, intense, one-of-a-kind sex – she was having a hard time convincing herself of that anymore.

She wanted him with every fiber of her being and the fact that she couldn't have him seemed like a cruel joke.

How long would they be able to keep this up, she wondered sadly. How long before their time apart outweighed their time together?

Once the semester began, what little free time she had now would disappear. Mel was an exceptional student, but she wasn't naive enough to think the degree would be easy. She'd have to work her ass off if she wanted a good position when she graduated.

But she'd wanted this weekend. She was even wearing the cherry red bustier. No, not wanted. She needed it. Needed to see Tristan and reassure herself that he was real.

Because nothing seemed real anymore. When they were together, she felt like an entirely different person. It wasn't that Tristan changed who she was, exactly. It was more like he opened her up to a side of herself that she'd never considered before. And Mel loved this hitherto unexplored sensual side, this woman inside of her, begging to be let free. Begging Tristan to let her free.

But when they were apart, it all felt like a dream. An amazing dream she never wanted to wake up from.

Mel called Tristan, and when he didn't pick up, she left a message telling him she was stuck in Princeton for the weekend. She sighed as she hung up. She'd at least hoped to hear his voice, even if it was only for a moment.

She'd been looking forward to seeing him. Instead, she

replayed her last visit to New York. She'd arrived sweaty and unkempt, wanting nothing more than to take a shower, but Tristan had just said no, telling her to get undressed.

"Tristan, I smell," she'd protested.

"Mel, I love the way you smell," he'd said fiercely. "I want to lick the sweat off you. It's so fucking sexy."

Mel lifted her arms above her head, stretching out, feeling the familiar tingle spread through her body as she thought of Tristan. Thank God, Professor Taylor had already left because right now, Mel didn't think she could hide her arousal from her boss. And she couldn't think of anything more mortifying than her seventy-year-old boss catching her fantasizing about sex.

But sometimes, she just couldn't help herself. The way Tristan had crossed his arms over his chest, daring her to disobey. The way he'd watched her in silence, his eyes scorching her flesh, until her clothes were piled on the floor and she was standing before him in nothing but her panties and pumps.

"You're fucking perfect," he'd whispered, letting his eyes slowly trail over every inch of her.

Just the way he looked at her, like she was the most beautiful woman in the world, made her pulse quicken and her skin flush.

"Take off your panties but keep the shoes on."

She'd nodded obediently, hooking her thumbs in the waistband and easing her panties down her thighs, kicking them aside with mounting impatience.

"Tristan," she'd started but he shook his head.

"Go into the living room. I want you kneeling on the floor with your legs spread wide for me. I'll be there in a minute."

He'd made her wait. God, he'd made her wait. Each second had felt like an eternity as she knelt on the rug, feeling the rough fibers dig into her knees and the cool air on her exposed sex. By the time he'd finally sauntered in, she'd been on the verge of screaming. Instead, she bit her lip and waited in silence.

Before Tristan, Mel never would have considered herself sexually submissive, but then, she'd never been with anyone remotely like Tristan. She loved the way he took control. The way he yanked her hair when he kissed her. The way he demanded every inch of her.

With Tristan, nothing was too taboo. Nothing was forbidden. And just the thought that anything was possible made Mel hot and needy.

She let her hand brush over her straining nipples before glancing nervously at the door. Professor Taylor wouldn't be back until Monday. It was a Friday night and Mel was probably the last person still in the building. She was fine. No one would come in.

Mel sighed, letting her hand trail down her side, sending a shiver down her spine as she remembered the look on his face. That possessive pride as he'd watched her, his hands shoved in his pockets, his erection visible through his pants. The thought that she made that gorgeous man lose control left Mel speechless.

She slipped her fingers beneath the hem of her dress, trembling as she brushed her inner thighs, letting her legs fall open. He'd looked at her for a long time, his mouth set and determined, before telling her that he needed to fuck her perfect little mouth.

She'd never thought a man speaking to her like that

could be such a turn on, but God, was it ever.

Mel found the damp patch at the center of her panties and rubbed her sex through the slippery fabric, feeling a jolt of electricity as the smooth satin brushed her overly sensitive clit.

"Clasp your hands behind your back," Tristan had growled. Mel did as he asked, pushing her breasts forward, and he wrapped his fist in her long hair, forcing her to meet his eyes as he teased her lips with the head of his cock. Mel could taste the pre-cum on the tip of his cock, making her ache for more. But there was nothing she could do but kneel there, helpless, panting, waiting for him to decide when he'd take her mouth.

It had been torture. Pure, delicious torture.

Mel's lips fell open as she stroked her clit and she sucked in a shallow breath. She needed to come. If she couldn't have Tristan tonight, at least she could have this. She eased her panties to the side, sliding one finger into her hot, wet sex, fucking herself with abandon. She was too far-gone to care where she was. She needed to release the tension that had kept her teetering on the edge since Tristan had made her go shopping. She squeezed her eyes shut, imagining Tristan on his knees, spreading her thighs, his hungry lips on her sex as he sank a finger into her...

The shrill ring of the phone brought Mel crashing back to reality and she yanked her hand away.

She sucked in a ragged breath, trying to steady herself before answering.

"What are you doing?" Tristan's husky voice vibrated through Mel's agitated body.

"Nothing," she lied shakily, hearing Tristan tsk in disapproval on the other end of the line.

"Mel, what did I say about lying to me?"

Mel shuddered at the sound of his voice, the playful reprimand that held so much promise. "That you'd punish me," she whispered with excitement, glancing once more at the door, almost expecting to see Tristan standing there.

Tristan chuckled. "Let's try that again. Mel, what are you doing?"

CHAPTER THREE

"Put me on speaker and lock the door," Tristan said sharply, leaving no room for discussion.

With shaky movements, Mel did as he asked, never once thinking about disobeying. She loved this side of Tristan. Demanding. Powerful. In control.

"Go to the window."

Mel moved in a daze. Outside, a light breeze ruffled the leaves of the mature trees lining the quad. The scenic campus was so at odds with the riot of feeling rushing through Mel's body.

"Is there anyone outside?"

"No."

Tristan chuckled, the sound like a match to Mel's body, igniting every inch of her skin. "That's a shame. I can't tell you how hard I am thinking about a stranger watching you come for me."

Mel squeezed her eyes shut.

"Why were you touching yourself?" Tristan asked, all playfulness suddenly gone from his voice.

Mel shivered. "I was thinking about you."

"Mel," he chastised and she knew exactly what he wanted. He wanted more. He wanted everything.

"I was thinking about the last time I saw you," she said, her voice trembling. Not with embarrassment but with arousal. Her sex throbbed, begging for her touch, but she knew better than to touch herself without Tristan's explicit permission.

"More, Mel. I want details. I want to know what made you feel the need to touch yourself at work."

Tristan's voice was rough with desire, and she sighed, relieved that she wasn't the only one this was affecting.

"I was thinking about the way you made me kneel and wait for you. I wanted you so badly, but you made me wait. I was thinking about how much I loved sucking your cock."

Tristan inhaled sharply and she wondered if he had his hand wrapped around his magnificent cock, stroking himself as they spoke.

"I can't wait to feel your lips tight around me. I love fucking your perfect little mouth."

Mel licked her lips nervously.

"Are you touching yourself?"

"No."

"Good girl. You don't get to come until I say so. Does Professor Taylor have a ruler on her desk?"

Mel felt the hairs on her neck prickle as she turned around, her eyes scanning her boss' desk. She knew what was coming and as much as she hated to admit it, even to herself, it excited her. "Yes," she whispered breathily.

Tristan laughed. "Get it. You need to remember what happens when you lie to me. I want you to slap your ass with it. Hard. Mel, I want to hear it."

Mel shivered, glancing out the window at the lush green campus. If anyone looked up, they'd see her, framed in the window. Which was exactly what Tristan wanted. Mel, on display.

"One palm flat on the window. Keep your eyes open. I don't want you to forget where you are."

Mel bit her lip as she held the ruler in her hand. She sucked in a deep breath and brought it down as hard as she could, the deafening crack making her yelp in surprise.

"That's it. God, I'm so fucking hard. I can't wait to fuck you. Do it again. Imagine I'm the one holding the ruler. Do you think I'd go easy on you, Mel? You're mine. And that means you don't masturbate at work unless that's what I want. Now do it again."

Mel gasped as a sharp sting radiated across her ass. Her whole body was on fire. Her pussy tingled. She was so wet.

"That's my girl," Tristan whispered, his words a calming balm to Mel's frazzled nerves. "Tell me, how do you feel?"

"I need you to fuck me," Mel whined, all pride erased by need.

"Baby, I'll fuck you soon, I promise. Do it again. Harder. I want to hear you scream."

Mel couldn't help the moan that escaped her lips. She was frustrated, on edge, in need, and she knew Tristan would keep toying with her until she was about to burst. She pressed her lips together, bringing the ruler down again. Her skin prickled, burning, and she squirmed, trying to find relief.

"Tristan, please..." she begged.

"Once more, Melanie."

Mel's pussy clenched in frustration, but she did as he said.

By the time Tristan finally told her to put the ruler down, Mel's legs were shaking and she was struggling to keep herself upright. Awareness coursed through her body.

"Please, Tristan, I need to come."

"Baby, you can touch yourself." His deep, husky voice was all the encouragement that Mel needed and she reached a trembling hand between her legs, amazed to find she'd soaked through her panties.

"Tristan…" she moaned, sliding a finger into her swollen sex, feeling her pussy clench down, begging for more. She added another finger as she fucked herself, her mind going blank as she focused on the heat radiating through her body.

"Taste yourself. Suck your fingers clean. Let me hear how much you love the way you taste."

Reluctantly, Mel withdrew her fingers and brought them to her lips as she stared out the window, slurping noisily.

"That's it. That's my girl."

Mel stumbled home in a daze. Her whole body felt heavy and drugged. She brushed her hair from her face, catching the unmistakable aroma of her sex on her fingers. She couldn't believe Tristan had cruelly deprived her of the one thing she craved above all else: release.

Just when she thought he would push her over the edge, telling her to come for him, demanding her release, he'd told her to stop.

"Melanie," he'd said sternly, "don't even think about coming."

Mel shuddered. No matter how much her body had screamed for more, she couldn't imagine disobeying him.

After that, there hadn't been much point remaining in the office. She'd try to get as much reading done tonight and then if she was lucky, she could take the train up to the city tomorrow. Because after this afternoon, Tristan owed her.

Mel cut across campus towards her apartment. She'd managed to find a one-bedroom on the ground floor of a beautiful Victorian a twenty-minute walk from campus. It was small but tidy and she'd been sold the moment she saw the wood-burning fireplace in the living room. Not that she could even contemplate having a fire going with the unrelenting summer heat. But she could imagine fall evenings sitting in front of a fire, sipping a glass of red wine while she read. As much as she tried not to, she always imagined Tristan with her, handsome and perfect in a woolen sweater, his feet up on the coffee table.

Mel shook her head, trying to banish the thought. No good would come from imagining nights like that, not with Tristan. He'd made himself perfectly clear – he wasn't looking for a girlfriend. And Mel had too much to lose if she fell any harder.

By the time she rounded the corner, her hair clung to the nape of her neck and she couldn't wait to get inside and open an icy cold beer. She dug impatiently through her bag, searching for her keys, her brow furrowed in concentration. A cold beer and a cold shower sounded perfect. It wasn't until she'd started up the front steps that she looked up and saw him, like something out of a dream, leaning casually against the banister with an overnight bag at his feet. Tristan looked up, giving her a lazy smile and for a moment, she hesitated, afraid that if she spoke, he'd disappear.

"What are you doing here?"

Tristan shrugged his broad shoulders, giving her a playful grin. God, he was gorgeous. "I was on the train when I called earlier. I have to say, it made for a very memorable trip." Tristan pushed off the banister, striding towards her. He pulled her into a deep kiss, his tongue finding hers as she grabbed a handful of his dark hair, holding him fast. With a quick movement, Tristan lifted her effortlessly and Mel wrapped her legs tight around his waist.

He brushed the damp hair from her face. "God, I needed to see you."

Mel threw her head back, laughing. "You needed to see me? How the fuck do you think I feel?"

Mel tossed her dress on the bedroom floor and Tristan growled when he saw what she was wearing underneath. Normally, he couldn't give a fuck about lingerie. It was just window dressing when he was interested in what lay beneath. But God, the way that cherry red satin stood out against her pale skin…it made him crazy.

"Did you come?" he rasped, watching Mel's expressive green eyes light up and she shook her head quickly.

"No."

Tristan couldn't help but smile at her proudly, knowing just how close she'd been. It was cruel of him, but he sometimes he couldn't help himself. He needed to reassure himself that he still had control of the situation.

He let his eyes roam her soft curves and perfect body. He wouldn't have blamed her if she hadn't been able to resist the temptation. Still, he was impressed.

"I think you deserve a reward after that." Even as he said the words, Tristan had to wonder who was really in for a reward. Because the idea of pleasuring Mel, of watching her come apart, knowing he was responsible for the look of wild abandon in her eyes was all the reward he needed. Tristan stalked towards her and Mel took a step back, hitting the bed and toppling onto the mattress.

Tristan was on her, his lips finding her skin, kissing and suckling. His mouth closed around one nipple and he gave it a teasing bite before releasing it. Slowly, he kissed his way down her stomach, feeling her tremble beneath him. He lapped the salt off her smooth skin and it made him wild. He liked her like this. More than liked. He didn't want his woman to smell like flowers or perfume. He wanted to smell her. That natural perfume that was pure woman. And God, did he love the way Mel smelled.

His fingers slid under her panties, dragging them down with agonizing slowness, exposing her wet sex to his hungry mouth. He inhaled deeply. God, she smelled amazing.

"Mel, I want to taste you. And then I want to tie you up and fuck you until you can't stop screaming," he murmured, nibbling the tender skin of her inner thighs, making her hips buck off the mattress. He couldn't wait to bury himself deep inside her, fucking her until he had his fill. Not that he ever seemed to be able to get enough when it came to Mel.

"I went to the Health Center last week like we talked about," Mel said breathily. Tristan looked up sharply.

"And?"

"No more condoms." The sweet smile that Mel gave

him made Tristan want to explode.

"Fuck," he growled, crawling up her body. "I'm sorry. I can't wait. I'll take care of you after, but right now, I need to feel you." He couldn't remember the last time he'd fucked a woman without a condom, couldn't remember the last time he was willing to take the risk, but Mel was different. She was nothing like the women he'd been with in the past. And the idea of being inside of her for the first time, without a condom, drove him wild.

He found her lips, kissing her deeply, loving the way her body moved beneath him with growing restlessness. She tilted her hips, tempting him, urging him to fuck her. He broke away, breathing hard.

"Turn around and get on your hands and knees," he bit out, stripping quickly. Mel glanced over her shoulder, giving him a coy smile that he felt deep in his gut. He let his eyes trail over her skin, and when he saw the red markings on her pale flesh, he groaned, running his fingers tenderly over them.

"Jesus," he sighed, sliding his fingers between her legs, finding her wet and ready. The image of her, leaning against the window, slapping her own ass with the ruler, was too much. He stroked her clit roughly before grabbing her hips and plunging into her quivering sex. Her tight wetness hugged his cock to perfection, and it was all he could do not to come right then.

"Play with yourself," he groaned. "I'm not going to be able to last and I need to feel you come apart on my cock."

CHAPTER FOUR

The evening air was warm and still as they sat on the front porch steps, drinking beer, watching the occasional firefly momentarily illuminate the quiet residential street. Mel sat between Tristan's thighs and rested her head against his chest and he wrapped one arm around her waist, pulling her tight against him.

"Thank you," Mel said softly.

"For what?"

"For being here." For the first time in weeks, she felt completely at ease and she knew Tristan was to thank for that.

Tristan kissed her shoulder, his lips dancing across her skin until they found the curve of her neck. "Where else would I be?"

Mel smiled. She never doubted their powerful sexual connection, but she worried she was in too deep. That she needed this more than he did. They hadn't discussed their relationship and for all Mel knew, Tristan was only interested in sleeping with her. The thought terrified her.

Tristan's fingers found hers, twining them together, the simple gesture immensely calming.

"So, Mary Taylor is working you to death?"

Mel found herself laughing. "Working me to death might be a bit of an overstatement, but yes, she's certainly keeping me busy."

"You could have stayed in New York and worked for me," Tristan said, nuzzling his face into her neck.

"Don't you think it's a little late to be mentioning that?"

"Would you have said yes?"

Mel shook her head, all the while knowing that if Tristan had asked her to stay in New York this summer, she would have. It would have been a mistake and she would have made it in a heartbeat.

Mel rested her head on Tristan's shoulder, amazed by how easy this felt. How natural. Sitting on the porch, sipping beers after a long, hard fuck. Mel could still feel his slick release on her inner thighs. Letting him come inside her had felt so different. At once intimate and primal. She'd never wanted a man to come inside her before, but Tristan wasn't just any man. He felt familiar. He felt like home.

It wasn't a feeling Mel was used to. She hadn't felt like she'd really had a home in a very long time. Probably not since she was a kid. Sure, she'd liked Seattle, but it was always a placeholder, the city where she ended up during that transition period when she was deciding what to do with the rest of her life. Looking back, she realized how impermanent it had always felt. She'd had a boyfriend and they'd shared an apartment and he'd talked about getting a dog, something big that they could take on hikes, but that wasn't the life she'd wanted. On paper, everything had been perfect.

It had taken her a while to admit it wasn't what she wanted, but when she realized it, she left Colin. He couldn't give her what she wanted or what she needed. Not that she knew what either of those things were. She just knew he wasn't it. And that life in Seattle, while it had been comfortable, it wasn't for her.

Sitting here, feeling the humid air on her skin and Tristan's arms wrapped protectively around her waist, she could imagine a future for the first time. And it scared her.

Because Tristan wasn't looking for a future. He wasn't looking for more than this. And at some point, she knew this wouldn't be enough for her.

Tristan ran his fingers lightly up and down her forearms, drawing her back to the present. He leaned in close, his warm breath fanning her neck and whispered, "Whatever you're worrying about, stop. Tonight, it's just you and me."

Mel nodded, wishing it were that easy. But it was never that simple. Neither one wanted to mention that the distance was a problem, but it was obvious. And Mel wondered if it was really something they'd be able to work out. Or worse, if it was really something that Tristan would want to work out. She'd always thought long distance relationships were insane, but she'd never met anyone worth making the effort.

Until now.

"Can I ask you something?" Mel asked hesitantly.

"You can ask me anything." Tristan pressed his lips to the base of her neck, making Mel wiggle closer, trying to erase any distance between them.

"Why did you want me to get that girl's number?"

Mel felt Tristan tense behind her and she wished she could turn around to see the expression on his face, but she was trapped in the cage of his arms, immobilized.

"Do you want to sleep with other people? I know with the distance and everything and we haven't exactly talked—"

Tristan's arms tightened fiercely around her waist, hugging her flat against his chest. "You think I want to sleep with other people?" Mel cringed at the barely suppressed anger in his voice. "Jesus Christ, Melanie, no. Absolutely not. You're the only person I want to sleep with and I hope to God you feel the same. Because I have no intention of sharing you."

Mel was shocked by his vehement response. She'd thought that he'd probably suggest an open relationship at some point. It only seemed reasonable. Even though after Tristan, Mel couldn't imagine ever wanting someone else. "Then why did you have me do it?"

Tristan let out weary sigh, his grip on Mel never relaxing and she could feel his steady heart beat. "Maybe this makes me a Neanderthal, but I wanted to know if you would." Mel felt Tristan shrug. "I want you to explore your sexuality with me. If that means sleeping with a woman, okay. But there's no chance I'd let another man fucking touch you. As far as I'm concerned, I'm the only man allowed anywhere near you."

Mel couldn't help but laugh. At times, he was so possessive. And yet, Mel knew exactly how he felt. Because the idea of Tristan with another woman made her sick to her stomach.

"I'll admit, it turned me on," he added, his voice

softening slightly. "Thinking about you hitting on that woman. It made me so hard knowing you were doing it because I asked. That you were thinking about me when you were with her."

Mel's shoulders dropped in relief. If Tristan had said he wanted them to be in an open relationship, she didn't know how she would have reacted.

"It turned me on, too," Mel admitted softly, remembering how wet she'd been, how uncertain and yet, empowered she'd felt. Tristan's erection stirred as she ground her ass firmly into him.

"Tell me, is it something you want to try?" he asked, sucking her earlobe into his warm, wet mouth, making Mel moan softly. "Do you want to fuck a woman while I watch? While I tell you exactly what to do?"

Mel felt a shiver of excitement shake her body as a warm glow spread through her. She felt hazy, uncertain. It wasn't that Tristan's words shocked her. Nothing he said could shock her now. She'd come to expect the unexpected from him. That was just one of the things that she loved about him. That he always kept her guessing.

Mel thought for a moment, before shaking her head. "I don't know."

"All you have to do is ask," he said, his words a dark promise. "I can't promise I'll agree to everything, but I want to know. I want to know what turns you on. I want to make this amazing for you."

She took one last look across the street before draining her beer. She'd had enough talking for one night. "Are you ready to go inside?" she asked. Because if he was only in town for the night, she had every intention of taking advantage of the time they had together.

Tristan let out a low chuckle and stood, reaching down and pulling Mel to her feet. Even in heels, she had to tilt her head back to meet his eyes. His beautiful face was covered in a wash of dark stubble while his eyes glittered in the glow of the porch light.

"I'm always ready when I'm with you," he whispered without a trace of irony, never once taking his eyes from hers. "I want to hear you scream out so loud it wakes the fucking neighbors."

Wordlessly, she took his hand, brushing it across her straining breasts and guiding it down her belly, under her skirt until it was at the juncture of her thighs. She pressed his hand into her naked sex, letting him feel just how turned on she was. He growled, a look of pure satisfaction breaking across his face as he dipped one finger into her pussy, stroking her tenderly.

"God, I've missed your beautiful cunt," he exhaled, penetrating her with agonizing slowness as they stood on the front porch of her house, neither one moving. Mel's lips fell open as Tristan brushed his thumb across her clit, but she never took her eyes off his.

"Should I make you come right here? Where everyone can see you? Do you want your neighbors to see what an insatiable little creature you are whenever you're with me? Is that what you want?"

Mel moaned, incapable of forming a coherent response. She didn't know if that was what she wanted or if what she really wanted was for him to hoist her into his arms and throw her down on her bed and take her. Take her rough and hard and unrelenting, making her body his. Because she was his. All of her. And she wanted to feel that possession.

Mel shuddered as Tristan continued rubbing her clit with increasing insistence, watching her crumble before him. Sensing her uncertainty, Tristan's lips smashed against Mel's, stifling her moan as he took her forcefully, his fingers never slowing.

Just as Mel felt the first delicious stirrings deep within, he broke away, letting his hand drop from her pussy and she let out a sigh, unsure if it was relief or disappointment that she was feeling, but Tristan didn't give her a second to think. He grasped her ass firmly in his large hands, lifting her with ease and she wrapped her legs around his waist, hugging herself to him.

"We can give your neighbors a show another night. Right now, I need to be inside of you again and I don't want a goddamned audience."

CHAPTER FIVE

Tristan watched Mel sleep, her face perfectly relaxed against the pillow. He couldn't believe he'd made her think, even for a second, that he wanted them to be in an open relationship. Just the thought made him sick to his stomach. Mel was his. Only his. And while the thought of Mel with a woman made his dick twitch with excitement, he didn't honestly believe he could go through with it, no matter what he'd told her last night. He had no interest in sharing her. With anyone.

He hated admitting it, but she consumed his thoughts. At work, at home. She was everywhere and he couldn't escape. Even if he wanted to. And he wasn't even sure if he wanted to.

He hated how helpless she made him feel almost as much as he hated being away from her. He still couldn't believe that she hadn't just walked out of his living room that night in April when he told her what he wanted from her. Her body. Her submission. He'd expected her to bolt and instead she'd held her ground, pushing back at him.

He reached over, brushing a lock of auburn hair from her face. She stirred, scrunching her eyes shut as she stretched out, but she didn't wake. Instead, she rolled towards him, nuzzling into his chest. He scooted down, careful not to disturb her, and placed his arm around her shoulders, stroking her skin as he thought. Just being here with her, watching her sleep, was all he needed to remind him that it was worth it.

He didn't know what they were doing, but he knew that he couldn't let her go.

He knew he should tell her why he was really in Princeton, but he didn't want to get her hopes up. Nothing was certain and he wanted to enjoy this time together, without looming concerns about the future. Because it was always there, the future, taunting them. He'd seen it in Mel's beautiful green eyes, that uncertainty he wished he could banish, but there was nothing he could say that would assuage her fears.

He let his fingers trail down the ridges of her spine, gathering her closer and letting out a contented sigh. This was exactly how he wanted to wake up in the morning. It scared him to admit it, but it was true.

Mel took one look at the alarm clock on the bedside table and sat straight up, panicked.

"Why the hell did you let me sleep so late?"

Tristan cocked his head, watching her with amusement. "It's 9:30, not noon. You're fine," he said patiently.

She frowned in irritation and hopped out of bed, heading straight for the kitchen.

"Where do you think you're going?" The sharp edge to Tristan's voice made Mel pause and turn around.

"Coffee. I need coffee."

Tristan shook his head, pushing the sheets off, giving Mel a view of his perfectly formed naked body. She swallowed hard. How was she supposed to concentrate with him here? He strode towards her, his erection hard and proud against his flat stomach and he gave her a kiss on the forehead.

"Babe, if you want coffee, I'll make coffee. Because you aren't leaving this bed until I've had my fill of you."

"Tristan, I have to work," she protested feebly, feeling her resolve crumble as his erection pressed insistently against her belly. She could always work later.

"Not a chance, Mel. Today, you're mine. All mine. When I leave, you can work, but today I own you. And right now, that means bed." He released her with a firm look. When Mel didn't move, he slapped her ass, hard enough to make her yelp in surprise.

"I'm serious, Mel. Get back in bed. Let me take care of you."

CHAPTER SIX

Tristan leaned across the ticket counter, his broad back stretching the white t-shirt across his muscles and Mel had to admit, there was nothing sexier than a man in a well-fitted t-shirt. Especially when that man was Tristan Everett.

God, she wondered, would she ever get used to him?

Tristan turned slowly, giving her a playful smile that made her want to throw herself into his powerful arms and beg him not to leave. Beg him for just one more night.

This was bad. So bad. Mel was falling for him. Hard. No, she realized. She'd already fallen for him. And Mel couldn't think of anything worse. Because what would happen when he inevitably decided he'd had enough? Sure, there were moments when Tristan looked at her and she thought she saw a glimmer of something more in his expression. But then, just as quickly, it was gone.

Mel scowled. God, she wanted it to be just sex. She wanted to feel nothing for Tristan except desire. Physical, burning desire. But she'd have to be a complete fucking idiot to believe that was it.

But when Tristan looked at her like that, it was so easy to get caught up in the fantasy. That Tristan wanted something more. His gaze shifted and a crease appeared between his eyebrows.

"Amanda?"

The look of confusion on Tristan's face made Mel turn around and she felt her stomach drop. Standing in the middle of the deserted train station was one of the most beautiful women Mel had ever seen. She stood motionless, watching Tristan with a ghost of a smile, her hands casually shoved into the pockets of her black silk slacks. She looked expensive, Mel thought, not knowing how else to describe her. Like she belonged to a world Mel would never be privy to.

With a studied gesture, she removed her sunglasses.

"Well, I'll be..." she said, trailing off in a way that alluded to so much more.

Mel glanced back at Tristan, but his eyes were still locked on the mysterious Amanda. He looked like he'd just seen a ghost and Mel felt a wave of panic crash over her. She watched Tristan try to shake off his surprise, a smile appearing on his face. He strode past Mel, ignoring her completely and placed a familiar kiss on Amanda's cheek.

"God, how long has it been?" he asked, stepping back and running a hand through his hair as he examined her.

Amanda threw back her head, laughing. "You know exactly how long it's been," she teased, giving Tristan a playful shove.

Mel felt her anxiety building with every moment Tristan didn't look at her. She'd always known there were women in Tristan's past, but somehow Mel hadn't anticipated how much seeing one would affect her. If she'd wanted Tristan to stay earlier, that had nothing on how she felt now.

Mel watched Tristan, begging him with her eyes to turn and look at her, to remember she was standing right there, but his eyes remained locked on the stunning woman in front of him. Mel felt her heart breaking. This was it. This was the moment he realized he was done.

No, Mel thought, shaking her head. He'd told her last night he didn't want to sleep with anyone else. Maybe this changed everything, but she wasn't going to stand by and just watch it happen.

Mel cleared her throat. "I should go," she said stiffly, making Tristan turn and look at her.

He gave her a wane smile that did little to ease her mounting concerns. No, whoever this woman was, she clearly meant something to Tristan.

He turned back to Amanda, placing his hand on her shoulder. "Amanda, this is one of my former students, Melanie Potter. She's a PhD candidate here. I was lucky enough to run into her." The lie left his lips easily and Mel forced herself to smile as she looked up at the statuesque beauty, desperately trying to pretend that nothing was wrong.

And in that moment, she wondered if she should be worried that Tristan could lie so fluently.

"It's good to meet you," Mel said, extending a hand. She could feel the other woman's sharp brown eyes watching her curiously. She didn't like the way she was looking at her. Like she was assessing the competition. Mel had zero interest in competing for Tristan's affection. Still, she wished she could take his hand, establishing once and for all that he was hers. Because the way this woman looked at Tristan, it was like she wanted to eat him alive. Instead, Mel crossed her arms over her chest and waited for Tristan to say something.

"Amanda and I were at Harvard together," Tristan explained and it was clear that he was just as uncomfortable with the situation as she was. And somehow, seeing Tristan, who was usually so in control, look uneasy made Mel all the more nervous.

"Tristan thought he was the best in the class but I made sure to knock him down a few notches," Amanda quipped, the affection clear in her voice.

"Amanda made sure I had to work for everything I got."

"There's nothing wrong with a little healthy competition. Keeps you sharp."

"That is does."

Amanda looked like she was about to add something when Tristan interrupted. "Let me walk Melanie out and we can talk on the train," he said quickly, putting an end to the conversation and Mel couldn't help but wonder what he was trying to keep from her.

Mel walked stiffly beside him, acutely aware of the distance he maintained between them, as though he were putting on a show for Amanda, one to prove that Mel was nothing more than a former student he'd run into. They stepped into the balmy night air and Mel took a deep breath, trying to steady her nerves. She didn't like that seeing that woman had her so unsettled.

"I'm sorry," Tristan said, reaching out to brush the hair from her face and thinking better of it, his hand dropping in midair and Mel watched with increasing panic as he shoved his hand into his pocket and glanced towards the door.

Mel tried to hide the hurt she felt. She knew he was just being cautious, but she didn't want to be his dirty little secret. Didn't want them to have to hide their relationship whenever they were in public. Not when she was falling in love with him.

Mel shook her head, trying to banish the thought. Whatever was happening between them, whatever feelings she had for Tristan, now wasn't the time to let him know.

Tristan looked down at her with dark, melancholic eyes. "God, you deserve better than this," he said finally, causing Mel's heart to beat even faster. For one impossibly long moment, she held her breath, afraid that he was going to tell her this was it.

Instead, he took a deep breath and said, "I wish I didn't have to go."

When Mel remained silent, Tristan reached out to brush a damp lock of hair behind her ear. "Are you okay?"

"How long were you together?" she whispered before she had a chance to think better of it. She wasn't usually jealous, but she'd seen the way they looked at each other. She wasn't blind.

He leaned down and brushed his lips against her cheek, his touch light and friendly. "We were together for a while in graduate school."

"Was it serious?" Tristan's vague answer did nothing to assuage her suspicions. Tristan, who was normally one of the most forthcoming people she'd ever met.

"Neither of us was looking for anything serious."

Mel frowned. "That's not an answer."

Tristan sighed wearily. "Yes, it was serious. But it's

been over since grad school. I haven't seen Amanda in almost a decade."

Mel stared into his eyes, desperate to believe him. Tristan glanced at his watch and cursed under his breath.

"Mel, I have to go. Please don't worry." He held her eyes a moment longer, letting his words sink in, before turning and walking back into the train station and Mel couldn't shake the feeling that she was losing him.

CHAPTER SEVEN

Tristan wanted to kick himself for leaving Mel like that. He'd seen the paralyzed uncertainty in her eyes. Like she was afraid he was walking away forever. How could he tell her he had no intention of walking away, ever? How could he tell her that what he felt for her was something he'd never felt for anyone else in his life?

But he couldn't have stayed without making Amanda wonder what exactly was going on between him and his one-time student. He sighed, lifting Amanda Hamilton's leather overnight bag and placing it above the seat before sliding in across from her, wishing he'd stayed behind. He should have stayed. He should have made sure that Mel understood that she had absolutely nothing to worry about. She deserved that much. Instead, he'd left because he was worried about what Amanda might think.

He was a complete fucking idiot, he thought, glancing at the woman sitting across from him. It didn't take a genius to realize why Mel reacted the way she had. Amanda was even more attractive than she had been when they were in school together. She'd grown into herself. Sophisticated. Elegant. Powerful. She was clearly a woman who didn't take shit from anyone and he'd always respected that about her. Even in school, she'd demanded respect and as a result, she was one of the most feared and sometimes even hated members of the English Department. But if she cared, she never showed it.

And Tristan, well, he'd respected her all the more for it. He liked a submissive woman in the bedroom, but outside, in the real world, he'd always been attracted to women who knew exactly what they wanted and weren't afraid to make enemies along the way.

No one had been surprised when they'd started dating. They were the rising stars of the English Department, and while they competed fiercely against one another, they never let it interfere with their relationship. In that way, they were the same.

Now, looking at her, he was surprised to find that all of the desire he'd once felt for Amanda had been replaced with nothing more than respect.

"I heard what happened," Tristan said carefully. "They're idiots for not giving you tenure." Academia was a small world filled with gossips and he'd heard about Amanda's recent rebuff.

Amanda shrugged, but Tristan knew her too well to believe it. She'd never taken rejection lightly.

"I have no interest in working with a group of men willing to overlook intelligent women based exclusively on gender," she responded dismissively.

"Is that what it came down to?"

She laughed. "Did you see the other candidate's CV? It was a joke. But he was a good ol' boy from a good ol' family." She shrugged again. "Fuck them. It doesn't matter if they come groveling later, I'm done."

Tristan nodded. She hadn't changed a bit. He was glad. It would have been a pity if age had mellowed her. "What are you planning to do now?"

"They want to keep me on as an associate professor, but I'm not interested. I'm applying for fellowships. One of them should work out."

"What happens if you don't get one?"

Amanda's lips curled into a biting smile. "Are you trying to tell me you don't think I will?"

The train jerked into motion.

"Not at all. I'm sure you'll land on your feet." He meant it. He had no doubt that Amanda would find another position. She was more than qualified.

When Tristan looked up, he caught her watching him carefully. He knew that look well. Whatever she was about to say, he wasn't going to like it.

"She's pretty," Amanda said finally. Tristan did his best to keep his expression neutral, but inside, he felt a stab of panic. There was a time when Amanda had known him better than just about anyone and he wasn't surprised that she'd seen through his bullshit about running into Mel. She knew his type. Intimately. "A little young, though, don't you think?"

When Tristan didn't answer, Amanda threw her head back and laughed. "Come off it, I'm not going to tell anyone." She put one elegant finger to her lips. "Your secret is safe with me."

"I appreciate that," he responded dryly.

Amanda watched him, her eyes wide with curiosity. "Don't tell me it's serious?"

Tristan shrugged. There wasn't a chance he was telling Amanda how he felt about Mel. It felt cheap. Especially when Mel probably still had no idea.

Amanda's eyes glistened with amusement. "God, look at you. I haven't seen you like this since you applied for your job at Columbia." She shook her head, clearly loving every second of Tristan's discomfort. "Be careful. Students are tricky."

"Speaking from personal experience?"

Amanda shrugged her shoulders, giving nothing away, and he wondered if there wasn't more to her story than she was letting on. It wouldn't be the first time that Amanda had slept with a student. There had been more than one undergraduate during her time as a TA. "All I'm saying is, you've worked too hard to throw it away for a piece of tail."

"She isn't a piece of tail," Tristan bit out, digging his nails into his palms as he struggled to control himself. Amanda gave him a condescending smile and shook her head, clearly enjoying herself.

"Well, if you're ever looking for a third, keep me in mind. I can recall a number of very memorable nights, you and me and a bottle of wine and some naïve girl willing to do just about anything to please you…"

Tristan growled which only made Amanda grin. She'd always enjoyed getting a rise out of him and she was one of the few people who knew how to push his buttons.

Amanda took one hard look at him and burst out laughing. "I'll take that as a no," she said, leaning back and closing her eyes. "That's a pity, I'm sure you've taught her well."

CHAPTER EIGHT

Tristan couldn't fall asleep. He didn't know if it was the look on Mel's face when he walked away or seeing Amanda that was keeping him awake. He hadn't seen her in over seven years. Not since he'd chosen Columbia over her.

He could still see the look on her face when he'd told her he'd gotten the job. They'd been in his apartment in Cambridge and she'd been wearing nothing but a pair of his underwear when he finally worked up the nerve. And for one brief and terrible instant, he'd thought she'd ask him to reconsider.

Instead, she'd laughed, saying he'd have been a fool not to take the position. At 28, they were too young to throw away professional opportunities for something as fleeting as romance.

At the time, he'd been relieved. Relieved and thankful. That they shared that outlook. That neither one was foolish enough to let love, or sex, impact their decisions, but now he couldn't help but pity those younger versions of themselves. They'd been too young to be so jaded.

Not that he regretted his decision. He'd made the right choice, though possibly for the wrong reasons.

After that, he'd sworn off relationships. He never wanted to be in that position again, where he had to choose between himself and another person. He knew most women wouldn't have reacted the way Amanda had that day. Instead, Tristan focused all his attention on his career.

Though Tristan was a sexual person, he could go long periods of time, perfectly content with what he was doing professionally. When he did need the company of a woman, there was always someone willing to agree to his terms.

But at 35, he had to wonder if maybe he'd been doing it all wrong. Every moment he spent with Mel made him realize just how starved he was for human connection. Not just sex, but something deeper. Something more basic. He spent entirely too much time alone. Working. Avoiding colleagues. Eating at restaurants with only a book to keep him company. Until meeting Mel, he'd never minded. But being with her, it had changed the way he viewed his life. For the first time in as long as he could remember, he felt lonely.

He groaned. He didn't want to tell Mel about the Emile Fellowship. Not because he wanted to keep secrets from her. But old habits were hard to break and he didn't want the uncertainty of the fellowship hanging between them.

More than that, though, he never wanted to put Mel in a position where she felt she had to choose between her career and him. It was obvious that she cared about him. Sometimes, when she thought he wasn't looking, she'd look at him with such admiration in her eyes that it took his breath away.

He wasn't an idiot. But he'd made himself clear from that start that he wasn't looking for something serious. He'd told her that all he wanted was sex.

Somewhere along the way that had changed.

Somewhere along the way he'd found himself falling for that perfect girl.

He groaned. He didn't know what to do. He knew they couldn't go on like this. He'd seen it in her eyes before he walked away. He wanted her to trust him. No, he needed her to trust him. And the thought that he could make her doubt them so easily worried him.

When he applied for the Emile Fellowship, he'd done it on a whim, figuring he'd make a decision once he heard back. Amanda hadn't said anything, but he knew she'd been in Princeton for an interview and suddenly, he realized just how much he needed the fellowship.

It would mean one year in Princeton. One year with Mel. After that, they'd know. Know if it was worth it. If they were worth it.

He wasn't ready to consider what his presence there would do to Mel. The impact it might have on her. She needed to focus. He knew exactly how demanding a PhD was. And she needed to concentrate. The last thing she needed was an insatiable man pawing at her constantly. He could tell himself all he wanted that he'd give her the space she required, but who was he kidding? He couldn't keep his hands off her. Just being in the same room made his dick swell with an unquenchable need. The only place he was satisfied was buried deep inside her.

Their sexual chemistry was something he'd never

experienced before and it took his breath away, even now, after two months. He needed her in a way that scared him, but for once in his life, he wasn't going to let his fear dictate his actions.

He tossed and turned, trying his best to sleep. If he got the position, Amanda could make things difficult for him. But some risks were worth taking, and all he had to do was think about Mel to know this was definitely one of them.

CHAPTER NINE

Mel threw herself back into work, trying desperately to forget about Amanda and the way Tristan had left. She couldn't believe the summer was almost over. In less than a week, Professor Taylor would leave for a two-week trip to the South of France, signaling the end to Mel's research position. She'd then have a week before orientation and she planned on spending every minute of that week with Tristan in New York.

Still, she couldn't seem to shake the way seeing Amanda made her feel. Insecure. Uncertain. She didn't want to be one of those women, overcome with anxiety whenever her man so much as looked at another woman. When Tristan told her there was nothing going on between them, she believed him. He'd never given her a reason to doubt him. From the start, he'd been completely upfront with her. That was one of the things that she loved about him. His complete, unflinching honesty.

But Amanda wasn't just anyone. She wasn't some woman Tristan had had an affair with years ago. Tristan, who'd made it clear he never dated, had been in a relationship with her. And Mel knew, for better or worse, you couldn't just forget your past.

When Mel came home from the office, she found herself perusing the Columbia University website. Tristan was the only reason she hadn't applied to graduate school there in the first place. The idea of spending five years studying with the man who had filled her thoughts and fantasies for years had sounded too overwhelming to even consider.

Now, she wondered if she'd made the wrong choice.

She'd received a fellowship that covered her tuition and helped with living expenses. Given how expensive school could be, she knew just how lucky she was. There was no way she'd be able to pay for grad school on her own. And Professor Taylor had all but told her she would mentor her, should she decide to focus her studies on Provencal literature. If she stayed, she'd receive an amazing education. She knew that. She just wondered what the price would be.

She sighed. She wanted to be with Tristan. Wanted to see what would happen. It would take her five years to complete her doctorate and there was simply no way they'd be able to sustain what they had for that period of time. Not living in separate cities.

Tristan had said nothing was wrong after he'd gotten back to New York but she could tell that something was bothering him.

Whatever it was, it didn't feel like nothing. It felt like everything between them was crumbling and it was all because they were apart. At least, she hoped that was the reason. She didn't want to consider the possibility that it had something to do with Amanda's unexpected appearance. Tristan would tell her if he wanted to stop seeing her. He'd tell her if there was someone else.

Mel bit her lip and grabbed her phone, dialing the number from the screen with trembling fingers before she had a chance to change her mind.

"Admissions Office, how may I help you?"

Mel cleared her throat. "I'm thinking of applying in the fall and I'm curious what requirements I'll need to meet."

"Fantastic. Let me put you on hold for one moment."

CHAPTER TEN

Every day that he didn't hear back about the fellowship, Tristan grew increasingly restless. He knew there was a good chance that he wouldn't get it. And then he'd have to make a decision. Could he really live without Mel? Was it worth it, putting them through this torture when they both knew it would end eventually?

Tristan clenched his fists in frustration. He didn't want to give her up. But he couldn't do this much longer. He'd seen the way Mel had looked at him at the train station and the last thing he wanted to do was hurt her. Though he suspected it was a little late for that now. He couldn't see a way around it. She'd gotten in too deep. They both had. That was never his intention. This was supposed to be easy.

There was no way they'd be able to continue like this. Her studies would suffer once the semester began. And he could already see the affect their relationship was having on him professionally. In class, he was distracted, a fact that wasn't lost on his students. Grading papers, he found himself having to reread entire paragraphs because he couldn't remember what he'd just read. The summer term had nearly killed him. It felt like he hadn't slept in weeks.

The only time he had a good night's sleep was when Mel was tucked in bed next to him.

Tristan sighed and went into the kitchen, looking for a bottle of wine. He needed a drink. Or ten. He just wanted to hear back from the fellowship, just wanted to know what decision he'd have to make. He felt physically ill thinking about walking away from Mel, but he knew it was the only way. It was only fair to her. She didn't need him dragging her down, not when she had so much promise. Maybe one day in the future, things would be different. But as things stood, they wouldn't be able to continue. He knew it deep down, he just didn't want to admit it.

He poured himself a large glass of wine and drained half of it quickly. He knew alcohol wasn't the answer, but he hoped it would at least take some of the edge off. He'd been staring at his phone for the past week and nothing. No word. He should have heard back by now, even if it was just to be informed that they'd given the fellowship to someone else.

Mel was finishing up work this week and then she'd come to New York. They'd get a few days together and then he'd have to tell her it was over. The timing was terrible. But what else could he do? He had to let her go. He needed to be the better man. If that meant letting the one person who mattered to him go, so be it. In the long run, she'd thank him.

Somehow, Tristan had a hard time believing that, but that's what he had to tell himself. Otherwise, he knew he'd never be able to go through with it. And he had to. This was about more than just what he wanted. This was about Mel's future.

Tristan was about to pour himself more wine when the shrill ring of the intercom interrupted him and he let out an impatient curse.

"What?" A wave of remorse washed over him. He was in a foul mood, but that didn't excuse barking at the doorman.

"Mr. Everett, there's a lady here to see you."

Tristan stood up straight, feeling a rush of excitement. Mel wasn't supposed to arrive until the following morning but maybe she'd been able to finish up work a day early.

"Send her up," he said roughly, before slamming down the intercom and striding over to the door. He felt a rise of excitement in his pants at the thought that for the next few days, he'd have Mel all to himself. If he had to let her go, he wanted to enjoy what little time they had left.

The elevator pinged noisily and the doors opened as Tristan leaned against the door, waiting, his chest beating hard. He couldn't wait to bury himself in her, to feel her pussy come apart around him, milking him to his finish. He couldn't explain the need he felt to mark her as his when he knew he was just going to let her go.

"What the hell are you doing here?" he asked in surprise.

Amanda smiled, looking him up and down. "I take it you were expecting someone else," she said, her eyes lingering on the bulge in his pants.

CHAPTER ELEVEN

Mel didn't know how Tristan would react when she told him that she was applying to Columbia in the fall, but she'd made her decision. She'd thought about calling him after she got off the phone with the admissions office, but in the end, she decided it would be better to tell him in person. Maybe she was rushing into it, but if she were honest with herself, she'd probably been in love with Tristan from the moment she stepped into his classroom over two years ago. It had just taken her this long to admit it.

Mel threw some clothes into her overnight bag and was nearly out the door when she stopped. She took one look at herself in the floor length mirror and shook her head, deciding to change. She wanted to wear the cherry red lingerie that Tristan had found so alluring the last time she'd seen him.

Maybe that way he'd be too distracted looking at her to react to her news. Because she wouldn't be able to take his rejection.

By the time Mel arrived in the city and made it up to Morningside Heights, it was well after eleven. She waved at Tristan's doorman as she walked through the enormous lobby towards the elevators, feeling a rush of excitement. She was nervous, but more than that, she was eager to tell Tristan. She wanted him to know exactly how she felt. She wanted him to know that she was willing to do just about anything to make this work.

"Please don't call up," she asked the doorman. "I want it to be a surprise."

"Of course," he answered with a nod. She'd been in Tristan's building enough times over the summer that by now the doorman knew her.

Mel was on edge as she waited for the elevator to make its way to the twelfth floor. And in a brief moment of bravado, she reached under her skirt and pulled down her cherry red panties.

The door opened and Mel walked slowly to the door, knocking loudly. And then she stood, waiting, her panties dangling from her index finger and a coy smile on her face and held her breath, praying he'd be home. Because this would be extremely awkward if it turned out that he was out for the evening.

She heard Tristan's heavy footfalls and then the door swung opened and Tristan was standing there, a wallet in his hand.

From the living room, a familiar female voice called out, "Make sure they didn't forget the moo shoo pork!"

Mel's heart stopped. "Oh God, this was a mistake," she stuttered, her face turning the same color as the underwear in her hand. Sitting on the couch behind Tristan, sipping a glass of wine, her legs tucked comfortable beneath her was Amanda. She cocked her head, giving Mel a curious smile.

And in that instant, Mel felt her entire world collapse. How could she have been so fucking stupid? How could she have really thought that Tristan felt the same about her? She turned quickly, trying to hide her face. She knew how she must look. Shocked. Mortified. On the verge of tears.

Tristan grabbed her before she had a chance to turn away, his eyes wild and unfocused. "Mel, what are you doing here? I thought you were coming in the morning."

She stared up at him, feeling pinpricks at the corners of her eyes as she willed herself not to cry. She didn't want to be that girl. The one who fell apart. The one who begged the man not to leave her.

She wanted to at least walk away with her dignity intact.

She swallowed hard. "I wanted to talk to you about something," she said, hearing the slight quiver in her voice. Tristan's eyes narrowed but he didn't say a word and Mel rushed on, "You're busy. I should have called. I didn't mean to interrupt."

Mel tried to turn away, but Tristan's fingers held firm, forcing her to look at him. From the living room, Amanda watched them with growing interest, an amused smile on her lips. Mel looked away. Somehow, knowing that perfect woman was watching her humiliation made this all the more unbearable.

Tristan glanced over his shoulder, a look of realization crossing his features. "Jesus Christ, Mel, is that what you think is going on?"

Mel flinched. He sounded angry, unbelievably angry as he looked down at her in disbelief. "You think I'd sleep with her?"

Mel shook, refusing to meet his gaze and that was enough. Tristan cursed loudly under his breath.

"Amanda, I need you gone when I get back," Tristan screamed over his shoulder before propelling Mel into the elevator and letting out a heavy sigh. "How could you fucking think that?" he hissed.

CHAPTER TWELVE

Tristan clutched Mel's hand in his, afraid that if he let go, even for a second, she'd run. Not that she'd get far in those sexy as hell heels she was wearing. But she had that look. One he'd never seen before. Like she was about to bolt. And it terrified him. He glanced back at her, her face bathed in shadows and the dim light of the street lamps. She kept her eyes focused on the pavement, like she was ashamed. Tristan wanted to punch something, but he forced himself to keep moving as he all but dragged Mel towards Riverside Park.

When they reached the edge of the park, Mel yanked her hand from his and he finally came to an abrupt stop, his heart pounding wildly in his chest. When he turned to look at her, she was staring at him, her lips parted like she was about to say something but then thought better of it.

Tristan cursed, unable to believe how stupid he'd been. When Amanda showed up, he should have told her to leave. He should have told her that he was done with her. Because he was. They were over and they had been for years. There had never been a moment of doubt.

Instead, he'd invited her in and opened a bottle of wine. Thoughts of Mel had him thinking unclearly and he'd actually found himself thankful for the company. He thought they'd be able to catch up, as old friends. And he'd been surprised to realize just how easy it was to talk to her, even after all that time. There had been a time when Amanda was the most important person in his life and talking to her, he could remember why.

But seeing the pain in Mel's beautiful eyes, he realized just how much of a mistake it had been. Mel had made it clear at the train station that she felt uncomfortable with his relationship with Amanda. She may not have said it, but he'd seen it in her eyes. And if he'd been thinking clearly, he would have told Amanda to leave.

Mel pressed her lips together and collapsed onto a park bench, her face crumbling. "Are you sleeping with her?" she whispered, her voice so quiet Tristan almost didn't make out the words.

"No!" he shouted, startling an elderly couple taking their dog for an evening stroll. Tristan gave them an apologetic smile and then turned back to Mel, his voice softening. "No. Jesus, Mel. No. Absolutely not. How many times do I have to tell you, you're the only woman I want? Amanda stopped by to talk about work."

Tristan could feel Mel's eyes on him as she tried to decide if she believed him. She sighed, unballing her fist, and he caught a glimpse of the red satin crumbled in her hand and it broke his heart. He came to sit next to her, his hand covering hers, closing her fist with his.

"Mel, how could you possibly think that I'd ever want to be with someone else?" Tristan couldn't mask the hurt in his voice. He felt betrayed that she could think so little of him.

Mel shook her head, her auburn hair coming loose and spilling around her bare shoulders. She looked beautiful. And forlorn. And for the first time, Tristan realized just how small she was. How fragile. "I don't know."

"Mel, you need to trust me. I need you to trust me," he said softly, meaning every word.

"I do trust you," she whispered, but one look at her face made Tristan cringe. She sounded absolutely miserable.

He reached out, brushing her hair from her face, letting his fingers linger across her soft skin. At least this time she didn't pull away. "What are you doing here?"

Mel blinked, her eyes wide and unfocused. "I decided to apply to Columbia."

"What?" The word exploded out of Tristan's mouth and he regretted it the moment he said it.

Mel shrugged, suddenly embarrassed. All it took was one look at the livid expression on Tristan's face to make her realize just how mistaken she'd been. He didn't want her here. Why would he? Just because he wasn't sleeping with Amanda didn't mean he wanted their relationship to get any more serious.

Tristan took a deep breath, like he was preparing himself for something terrible, and Mel hunched her shoulders, waiting for him to tell her it was over. That he didn't want her. Not in New York and not in his life.

"You can't do that," he said slowly, his voice softening.

"Why not?"

"I'm not a safe bet, Mel. Don't jeopardize your future

on a gamble."

"What are you talking about?"

"Mel, I don't do relationships. I never have. Don't throw everything away on the hope that I'll become someone I'm not."

"You dated Amanda."

Tristan sighed. "That was different."

"Then what is this to you? Because it feels a hell of a lot like a relationship to me."

When Tristan didn't say anything, Mel felt the anger rising in her chest. All the words that she'd thought and kept to herself over the summer. All the feelings she'd wanted to share with him but had been too afraid to voice. Afraid that he'd tell her he didn't feel the same way about her. But there was no point in hiding any more.

"Are you telling me this is really just sex? That you don't feel anything more for me?"

A look of panic crossed Tristan's face. "Don't do this."

"Do what? Tristan, I love you. You'd have to be a fucking idiot not to realize that. I'm in love with you."

CHAPTER THIRTEEN

"Mel," Tristan started before trailing off. Mel could see the panic in his eyes even in the shadows of the park and she turned away, wishing she could take back the entire night. This wasn't how tonight was supposed to go.

She was an idiot. But at least it was out there. At least she was being honest. Because she couldn't go on pretending that this was just sex. Not when she was willing to throw everything away just to be with him. Tristan's silence was like a knife in her stomach, but at least she knew. This was it. She'd go home and pick up the pieces.

Suddenly, Tristan was wrapping his arms around her, hugging her tight against his chest. She tried to push him away, but he wouldn't let go. Eventually, she relented and she wrapped her arms around him, feeling his rapid heart beat against her cheek. She clung to him, her fingers digging into his back, afraid that if she let go, that would be it.

"I won't let you do this," he said fiercely, his grip never loosening.

"Tristan, this is impossible. We can't do this. I can't do this. I can't sacrifice my work because I need to see you all the time. And this worry about the other women in your life...I don't want to be this person. I fucking hate this person."

"I know," Tristan cooed as he stroked her back. "We'll figure something out. I promise. But you can't walk away from Princeton. Not for me."

He rocked her against his chest, stroking her, whispering in her ear.

Mel lost track of how long they sat on the park bench, hugging each other, but eventually, she let Tristan lead her back to the apartment. He never let go of her hand, and Mel felt oddly comforted by the touch. He didn't love her, but he wasn't pushing her away either. She didn't know what any of it meant, but it gave her some hope.

He squeezed her hand reassuringly as they stood next to each other in the elevator, but she kept her eyes on the linoleum tile, refusing to look at him.

Had she really thought he'd tell her that he loved her? Had she really thought it would be that easy?

Mel felt drained and she let Tristan lead her to the couch. He kneeled in front of her, easing her shoes off her aching feet. Mel stared at the glass on the coffee table, a smudge of plum lipstick on the rim and Tristan's eyes followed hers and he stood quickly, whisking away the glass and then returning once again to the floor in front of her. She looked at him, kneeling in front of her, a pained expression on his face.

This was the end. She knew it. But she was too tired to brace herself for the inevitable. Too tired to walk out the door with whatever dignity she had left.

"Mel, look at me."

Reluctantly, Mel lifted her face until she was staring straight into Tristan's wide, dark eyes. He rested his palms flat on her thighs, locking her in place. She could see the struggle in his eyes as he watched her, his lips parting, but he didn't say anything and Mel just turned away, closing her eyes. She couldn't look at him. Because every time she did, she saw that blank terror in his eyes when she'd told him that she loved him.

"Mel..." he whispered, but Mel refused to look at him. "Mel, you know how I feel about you," he tried again. When Mel didn't say anything, he let out a curse, coming quickly to his feet. "What do you want me to do? Jesus, Mel. I'm standing right in front of you. Of course I care about you. I'm willing to throw all this away, for you." He waved his arms frantically around the apartment. Mel stared at him in confusion.

"I should go," Mel said finally, struggling to her feet. She needed to get away, to find somewhere where she could think. And right now, there was no way she could think with Tristan standing in front of her, that look of heart break painted all over his face.

Tristan blocked her path, towering over her. "You aren't leaving. Not like this."

Mel sighed, pushing past him but he grabbed her wrist, forcing her to turn back to face him.

Tristan stared at her, his mouth hanging open, but no words came out and just as Mel was about to turn away and walk out the door, he grabbed her to him, pressing his lips to hers in a fierce kiss that knocked her off balance. Her hands found his chest, pushing against him, trying to push him away as his tongue took her mouth fervently, like a man who was starved. Gradually, she felt herself relaxing into his arms, giving into the sensual assault. She loved him. She loved him so much it hurt. And she hated herself for capitulating so easily to his touch, but she was helpless in front of him.

Tristan pulled back, keeping his hands firmly on Mel, his eyes wild. "Mel, I don't fucking deserve it. I don't fucking deserve you. But I do love you. I. Love. You." He pulled her into his chest and she could feel him press a kiss into her hair, murmuring sweet words that she couldn't make out.

Tristan gently tugged down Mel's zipper, exposing the long curve of her beautiful spine. He kissed his way down her back, pulling the dress down as he went and came to kneel behind her, his hands firm and gentle on her full hips.

Tristan knew he didn't deserve the woman standing in front of him, that he should thank his lucky stars every morning that she was even willing to be in the same room with him. He didn't fucking deserve her but he was too selfish to let her go. He pressed his lips to her ass, feeling her tremble in his arms.

Carefully, almost reverently, he helped her turn and when he looked up, he met her beautiful green eyes. He hated seeing her like this. Hating seeing this beautiful strong woman vulnerable. And worse, hated knowing that he was the reason she looked like she was about to fall apart in front of him.

He'd seen the frantic flash of doubt in her eyes when he told her he loved her. As if she was afraid he was saying those words just to pacify her when in truth, he'd never been so serious in his life.

He knew he had to prove himself to her. That he had to make her realize just how much he cherished her. He gave her a small smile before pressing his lips to the bare skin of her sex. She sucked in a shocked breath, and just hearing her made him hard, but this wasn't about him. Tonight was about Mel. About making her feel like the most beautiful woman in the world. Because she was. He couldn't imagine anyone more beautiful than the woman standing in front of him, vulnerable and yet willing to give herself to him.

God, he didn't deserve her.

"I could eat this pussy all night," he murmured, nuzzling her sex with his nose, breathing in her rich musk. With deliberate tenderness, he began licking and nibbling her slick sex, feeling her shudder around his mouth. "I love the way you taste. I love that you let me do this," he said, running his tongue the length of her cleft. He kept his hands firmly on her ass, steadying her as he fucked her with his mouth, slowly, lavishing her body with the attention it deserved. "I love the look you get when you come. I love the way you feel, right after you climax."

He gave her one long lick before coming to rest on his heels and looked up at her, his mouth glistening with her juices. He licked his lips, watching the spark in Mel's eyes.

"Mel, tell me what you want. Tell me what I can do. I'll do anything. Just tell me," he begged. Never in his life had Tristan kneeled before a woman and begged, but right now, there was nowhere he'd rather be. He needed this just as much as she did. He needed to reassure them both that they were okay.

And for once, this need he felt for Mel didn't scare

him. Instead, it filled him with an unexpected warmth that radiated from his chest. He pressed his lips to her clit, sucking it gently into his mouth, making her hips buck unexpectedly, but he held her firmly in place.

"Tristan," she shuddered around his mouth and when Tristan looked up, he noticed her eyes were closed and it took all his willpower not to demand that she look at him.

"Let me make love to you. Let me pleasure you. Please," he pleaded, his warm breath fanning her sex.

When Mel finally nodded, Tristan darted to his feet and lifted Mel easily into his arms. She was so delicate, it sometimes amazed him. That this beautiful, delicate creature was his. And the thought that he'd hurt her, that he'd made her doubt him, doubt them, even for an instant made him want to break something. Instead, he cradled her in his arms and carried her into the bedroom, placing her gently on the bed.

"Mel…" He kept his eyes locked on her as he quickly shed his clothing and crawled over her, his lips finding hers, her warm breath sweet and gentle on his lips. He kissed her mouth, kissed her jaw, his kisses moving gently across her skin. He felt her quiver beneath him, which only made him want to kiss every inch of her. He just hoped she'd believe how much she meant to him when he was finished.

Because after tonight, he would do everything in his power to guarantee that she understood, every day, just how much she meant to him. He sucked her nipple into his mouth and felt her arch off the bed, her body seeking his. Seeking him. And for a brief moment, Tristan thought everything would be okay. Just as long as they stayed like this.

He never stopped kissing her as he parted her thighs with a gentleness that surprised even him. He brushed his fingers along her sex, making sure she was ready. Mel moaned, squeezing her eyes shut and Tristan placed himself at her entrance, feeling her slick folds caressing his erection. He kissed her eyelids as he eased himself into her, feeling her shudder around him as she tilted her hips, drawing him even deeper.

Tristan couldn't help but moan. She felt amazing. This is where he wanted to spend the rest of his life. Deep inside her. Feeling the way her body responded to his.

He nuzzled her neck, placing soft kisses everywhere that his lips found. "I love you," he whispered as he began moving inside of her, feeling her come to life around him.

They would be okay, he reasoned. They had to be. Because this, right here, being in Mel's arms, felt like home.

Mel awoke with a panic in the middle of the night. For a brief moment, she didn't know where she was, all she knew was that she couldn't breathe. She struggled to sit up, but Tristan's arms were wrapped around her body, holding her in place. She could feel his steady breathing and she wiggled, trying to free herself.

"What are you doing?" Tristan mumbled as he pulled her even closer to him and Mel could feel his erection nudging between her legs, reminding her of the way he'd made love to her last night before she'd succumbed to exhaustion. She couldn't believe this was the same man.

"I can't breathe."

"Mmm," he murmured, his grip loosening only slightly as he nuzzled her neck. "Don't go anywhere, love, please. I need to hold you tonight. Please don't go."

Mel could hear the desperation in his voice and couldn't help but relax into his arms, comforted by the way they tightened around her and she closed her eyes. For tonight, she didn't want to think. She just wanted Tristan to hold her.

CHAPTER FOURTEEN

While Mel slept in, Tristan made a few calls, clearing his schedule for the remainder of the week. There wasn't a chance he was leaving Mel alone. Not after last night. He knew he was being ridiculous, but he still couldn't shake the fear that she might just walk out without saying a word. And he wouldn't be able to blame her if she did.

If he could go back to last night and re-do those panicked minutes where he'd just stared at her instead of saying he loved her, he would. He still couldn't believe he'd just sat there, mute, like a complete fucking idiot.

How could he tell her that he'd been too taken aback by her honesty to respond? That he'd panicked, not because he didn't know how he felt about her, but because he hadn't expected those three words to affect him so deeply. His entire adult life, he'd thought people were ridiculous for placing so much meaning in words, but he'd been wrong. God, he'd been wrong. Because hearing Mel say she loved him was the most moving experience of his life.

He just hoped she'd give him to the chance to prove it to her.

That didn't change the fact that he wouldn't let Mel walk away from Princeton for him. He didn't care what it would take, he'd figure something out. But not this week. This week was about reassuring them both that they were okay. And after last night, he knew just how desperately they needed it.

He couldn't believe he'd actually been considering ending things with Mel. There was no fucking way he was letting her go. If that meant quitting his job and moving to Princeton...well, he'd consider it. He'd been selfish his entire life, focusing exclusively on his needs, and he knew that phase was over. It was time to change his priorities. And right now, the woman asleep in his bed was his only priority.

He still couldn't believe three words could change everything but they had. There was no going back.

For a moment, he stood in the doorway, watching her sleep. She looked so beautiful, so peaceful, all the worries of last night erased. She must have been terrified when he hadn't said anything. He'd seen it in her eyes. The panic. The fear that she'd ruined everything. But right now, she looked perfectly content. A better man would let her continue to sleep, but Tristan was anxious to know that when she woke up, she wasn't going to change her mind and bolt.

"Good morning, sleepy head," he said, pressing his lips to Mel's forehead. She stretched out, her face scrunching in a way that was undeniably adorable. He sat on the bed next to her, stroking her hair out of her face. "I'm all yours. What do you want to do today?"

Mel smiled, rubbing the sleep from her eyes. "Coffee. I need coffee before I can think about anything else."

Tristan returned her smile. "Get out of bed. Coffee's all ready. But Mel, don't even think about getting dressed. When you're here, I want you naked. Always. There's no way the woman I love is hiding her delicious body from me," he said, loving the way Mel grinned at his words. Tristan knew exactly how she felt. Because he felt it too. Like his heart was going to explode.

"Picnic," Mel said finally. "This is my last week of freedom and I feel like I've been stuck inside all summer. I'm hideously pale."

Tristan frowned. "There's nothing hideous about you," he said with complete seriousness and Mel had to laugh.

"Joking. I'd just like to see a little sun. Do you think you'll let me put on clothing long enough to leave the house?"

Tristan pretended to consider his response. "I suppose that will be acceptable. But I don't see any reason why you'd need anything on underneath one of those sundresses you're so fond of wearing."

As they stepped into the elevator, Tristan took Mel's hand and he didn't let go as they walked down Broadway to a little neighborhood bakery to pick up lunch. If Mel wanted a picnic, he'd give her a picnic, he thought. He bought sandwiches and fruit salad and macaroons and two large iced teas and then they headed down to Riverside Park.

Sun filtered through the leaves of the trees towering over them, and Mel's auburn hair shone in the late afternoon light. She looked like an angel. Perfect. Untouchable. Tristan had to remind himself that she was real. Not only that, but she was his to touch. As long as he didn't fuck this up, again.

Tristan leaned back on one elbow, watching Mel eat. He wanted to memorize every detail about her. He was resigned to the fact that he wasn't going to get the fellowship. It wasn't ideal, but it didn't matter. They'd find a way to make it work. He loved her and he wasn't letting her go.

Mel wiped a stray crumb from her lips and glanced at him, giving him a funny smile.

"What?"

Tristan couldn't help but feel a flutter of excitement in his chest. "God, you're so fucking beautiful," he whispered fiercely, watching a blush come to Mel's skin. He loved the way she blushed whenever he complimented her. It just meant he'd have to keep on complimenting her.

Mel kicked off her shoes, stretching her toes in the grass and Tristan leaned over, running a finger along her sole, making her squirm.

"You have such lovely, little feet," he whispered, pulling her foot onto his lap and taking it in both hands, massaging it firmly. Mel's eyes closed and she leaned back, moaning with pleasure. He dug his thumbs into her delicate arches. Even her feet were beautiful, he thought, shaking his head. What the hell had happened to him?

For once, Tristan didn't give a shit. He'd become one of those sappy people he'd always looked at with contempt, but he couldn't care less. Not when it was because of Mel. He lifted her foot to his lips, pressing his lips to her skin. There wasn't a part of her body that he didn't love, he thought, before he closed his lips around her big toe, sucking it gently into his mouth, delighted by the gasp of surprise that escaped Mel's lips.

"What are you doing?" she shrieked, trying to yank her foot away. He loved the way she looked around nervously, afraid someone might have seen what he'd done. Tristan just grinned, refusing to release her foot. There was something so delicious about that look of fear laced with excitement in her eyes. It was the look she got whenever he pushed her out of her comfort zone, letting him know she liked it just as much as it scared her.

"Close your eyes and relax. I promise I won't do anything you object to." Just knowing she wasn't wearing anything under her dress made him hard, but he intended on teasing her.

Mel rolled her eyes but did as he asked, sending a wave of pleasure coursing through Tristan's body. He rolled his tongue around her toe before giving her a playful bite. There wasn't a single part of Mel's body he didn't want to lavish with attention. And he needed her to realize, if she was his, she'd have to get used to that.

The soft sound of Mel's moan made Tristan's dick twitch in his pants. Yes, she definitely liked this, he thought deviously. They were sitting in a deserted corner of the park. No one would notice. He continued suckling her, his hands gliding up her smooth calf and Mel just leaned back, letting him.

When he'd finished with that foot, he placed a kiss on her inseam before scooping her other foot between his hands.

"Tristan..." she pleaded, opening one eye as she stared at him.

He shook his head. "Mel, relax."

By the time they got back to the apartment, Mel felt like she was going to explode. She'd never thought something so simple could be such an erotic experience, but she'd felt it to her core. With her eyes closed, she imagined sucking Tristan's cock into her mouth right after he'd come, tasting them both on him as she lavished him with attention until he began to harden in her mouth. That thought, combined with the sensation of his warm mouth around her toes, made her wet and her nipples come to hard points.

Finally, she'd had to open her eyes and with a ragged breath insisted Tristan take her home. Immediately.

Tristan gave her his most devious smile and finally agreed, helping her to her unsteady feet. His innocent touch kept her on alert as they walked quickly back to the apartment.

Mel didn't even bother getting undressed. The moment the door slammed shut, she pulled Tristan to her, one hand freeing him while her other hand grabbed hold of his hair, yanking his head down to her mouth.

"You are a very cruel man," she murmured, coming up for air.

"And you love it," he responded quickly, making Mel's heart soar.

The week passed in a blur. Tristan kept his promise. He'd cleared his schedule and focused all of his attention on making sure Mel enjoyed every second they were together.

It was hard to believe that she was actually going back

to Princeton soon. Over the course of a week, everything had changed. She knew it should make everything easier when she left, knowing that they were okay, that they would find a way to make it work, but all it did was fill her with sadness. It felt so natural, the two of them together. And she didn't want it to end.

On her last night, Tristan insisted on taking her to dinner to Le Bistro Noir. It was the bar on Frederick Douglas Boulevard where they'd first gone out for drinks. That was the night when everything changed. It felt like a lifetime ago and she couldn't believe it was only April when she ran into him, a chance encounter that had set her life down a path she'd never imagined. She couldn't imagine her life without Tristan and the idea that she'd soon be in a different city filled her with a sadness she could barely hide from Tristan, no matter how hard she tried. She wanted their last night to be special. She wanted it to be happy, but whenever she looked at him, all she could imagine was what it would be like again, once they were apart.

It would be different this time, she knew, but that didn't change the fact that they'd be living in separate cities.

Tristan ordered a bottle of wine and an assortment of appetizers. Far more than either of them could possibly eat. Neither mentioned that Mel was leaving in the morning. Neither wanted to break the spell that hung over the table. That anything was possible. That this wasn't the end but the beginning.

Mel felt her unease rising as they walked silently back to the apartment. This was it. This was the end.

Inside, Tristan told Mel to go into the bedroom and

wait for him. This demanding words were enough to banish her fears, at least for the moment. Somehow, whenever Tristan took control, Mel was able to forget everything else except for the moment.

When Tristan came into the bedroom, he was holding a black paper gift bag. "I got you something," he said and Mel found herself smiling.

"You got me a present?"

"You could say that." He handed her the bag and sat next to her on the bed, resting his hand on her thigh. "I know this isn't going to be easy, but I promise you, we'll make it work. But I don't want you getting lonely when I'm in the city."

Mel glanced at him nervously. "Okay."

He nodded to the bag and Mel reached her hand into the tufts of neon pink tissue paper, her mouth dropping open when she saw what he'd gotten her. In her hand was a large, purple vibrator shaped like a cock. She ran her finger along its edge, glancing up at Tristan through her eyelashes.

"You bought me a vibrator?"

Tristan shook his head. "I bought us a vibrator. Whenever you come, Mel, I want you thinking about me. When you fuck yourself with this, I want you imagining it's my cock inside of you."

Mel nodded, her mouth suddenly dry. "Tristan…"

He shook his head. "We're going to make this work." He leaned in, kissing her fiercely and she could practically feel the heat radiating off him. She dropped the toy, running her hands through his hair, pulling him into her.

When Tristan pulled away, they were both breathing hard and Mel could feel the arousal between her legs, the need that filled her whenever she was with Tristan. She'd miss him when she was gone, but for the first time, she believed him. They'd make this work. Because there was no other option.

"Will you do something for me?" he asked, his voice rough and husky and she could see the arousal in his eyes, the way they lingered on her mouth. She licked her lips nervously.

"Okay."

"You're leaving tomorrow," he said slowly. "And I don't know when I'm going to see you next."

"Tristan, we don't have to talk about this now," she said quickly. The last thing she wanted to do was spend their last night together talking about a time when they wouldn't be able to see each other.

But Tristan shook his head. "Mel, I want to be able to watch you come every night when you're gone. I want to see that look in your eyes when you come apart. Will you let me film you? I promise, no one will ever see it but me. I just want to be able to fall asleep every night, knowing that I've heard you scream my name when you come apart."

Mel stared at Tristan. "Okay." The look he gave her made her heart race and she suddenly felt lightheaded. "What do you want me to do?"

"I want to watch you fuck yourself with that toy. And baby, when you come, I want you to scream my name."

CHAPTER FIFTEEN

Mel woke up, alone, in Tristan's bed. She blinked in confusion, taking in the bright morning light, shocked to see that it was almost ten. Her heart sank when she realized she had less than an hour before she had to go to Penn Station to catch her train. Orientation was the following morning and she'd pushed off leaving as long as she could.

"Tristan?" she called out, slipping out of bed.

"Stay right there," Tristan called out from the living room. When Mel came out of the bathroom she found Tristan sitting on the edge of the bed, a tray of pastries next to him. The delicious aroma of freshly brewed coffee made her stomach rumble.

He lifted a bottle of champagne. "Champagne?"

Mel tilted her head, letting out a short laugh. Her whole body still felt weak from the night before. After Tristan was satisfied with her performance on the video, he'd made sure that she was very, very satisfied. Mel blushed, just thinking about it. She couldn't believe he'd had her do that. No, she realized. She wasn't surprised. She just couldn't believe that she'd agreed.

"What is all this?" she asked suspiciously. Tristan wasn't really the breakfast in bed type.

He gave her a bashful shrug and used his thumb to ease the cork from the bottle with a subdued pop. "I didn't want to mention anything until it was finalized, but I got the fellowship."

Mel sat tentatively at the edge of the bed and picked up one of the chocolate croissants. "What fellowship?"

"The Emile Danner Fellowship," Tristan said slowly.

Mel took a bite of her croissant, wiping the crumbs from her lips. "Never heard of it."

Tristan lifted one eyebrow playfully. "Really?"

Mel nodded.

"Well, it's a very prestigious fellowship," he answered playfully, leaning over to kiss her temple. "It would mean I'd have to move, but I think it's a very good opportunity."

Mel's heart sank. "Move?"

Tristan nodded, smiling. "Yes, it would definitely make sense for me to move." Tristan poured her a glass of champagne and passed it to her. Mel took a sip, bracing herself for the worst. "It's a year-long fellowship. In Princeton."

Mel nearly spit champagne in Tristan's face. "What?" she sputtered.

"I start in a week."

Mel's eyes went wide as she stared at Tristan. This would be the most fucked up joke on earth if he was kidding. "You're serious?"

"I got the call this morning," Tristan said, giving her a smug smile that lit her whole body.

"Oh my God, that's amazing!" Mel squealed, throwing her arms around Tristan's neck. Tristan chuckled, prying Mel's fingers off and coming to his feet. There was a crease between his eyebrows and Mel felt a stab of worry.

"What's wrong?" she asked softly. She'd hoped and prayed all their problems were behind them.

"Melanie Potter," Tristan said solemnly, reaching into his pocket and pulling out a small box. He dropped to one knee and took her hand gingerly in his. "Melanie Potter, will you marry me?"

When he opened the box, Mel found herself staring at an enormous diamond ring.

PART THREE

CHAPTER ONE

Mel hurried across campus. She was definitely going to be late for her first class of the semester. Not that it was her fault. She held out her hand, admiring the diamond engagement ring on her finger. She still couldn't believe it. Couldn't believe Tristan had actually proposed. When he'd knelt by the bed, she thought her chest was going to explode. She remembered thinking it was all a dream, but the look in his eyes had reassured her: this was real. They were real.

Somehow, her fairytale had come true. Tristan was teaching in Princeton for the year. No more train rides back and forth. No more wondering if they'd be able to make the distance work. She still couldn't believe it. The man she'd wanted since he was her college English professor wanted to spend the rest of his life with her. Mel let out a sigh, pushing into the academic building. It was her first day of classes and late wasn't the impression she wanted to give. She wasn't the type of student to show up late. Ever. But it wasn't her fault that Tristan had held her captive in bed all morning. Her body still hummed with excitement. There hadn't been time for a shower and she could still smell the tantalizing mix of sex and Tristan on her skin.

Yes, it was definitely Tristan's fault she was going to be late for her first class of the semester. She stopped outside the classroom and considered the diamond on her finger, frowning. She hadn't taken it off once since Tristan slid it onto her finger, but they'd been living in a bubble, just the two of them. Eventually, they'd have to tell the university. After all, Tristan's fellowship had him teaching a class in the Comparative Literature Department. But for now, Mel thought it would be best not to draw attention to their relationship.

Reluctantly, she slipped the ring off, tucking it away in the zippered compartment of her purse.

It felt strange, being without the ring, even for a moment and she realized just how much she'd gotten used to wearing it during the past week. With a sigh, she pushed open the door, steeling herself for the apology she knew she'd owe Professor Ruiz.

All heads turned to her and Mel felt her heart sink when she looked at the front of the room. Standing in front of the blackboard was Tristan Everett, her Tristan, looking impeccable, his lips twitching into the slightest frown.

Her brow furrowed in irritation as she slid into a seat by the door. What the hell was Tristan doing here and where the hell was Professor Ruiz? The schedule had clearly stated that Professor Ruiz was teaching the Monday morning seminar on Postmodernism.

Tristan made a point of glancing down at the paper on

his desk before focusing his attention on Mel. "Miss Potter, nice of you to show up."

Mel tried her best not to glare. "Sorry, it won't happen again," she muttered.

Tristan tilted his head as he considered her. "No, I should hope not." His gaze left Mel and Mel sank down, momentarily relieved. This couldn't be happening.

But of course, it was.

"As I was saying." Tristan turned back to the rest of the class. "I'm sure each and every one of you is very smart. You got into this program. That said, this isn't an easy class. If you are looking to start off with an easy grade, I suggest you leave now instead of wasting my time. I expect the most from each of you and I assure you, if you fail to meet my requirements, I have no qualms with failing you."

Tristan let his eyes slowly roam the classroom, letting his words sink in. This was the man she'd fallen for as an undergrad. The man who refused to take any bullshit. The professor who'd inspired her to apply to graduate school.

When Tristan's eyes landed on her hand resting on her desk, Mel flinched. It was as if his eyes were burning into her and she knew instinctively that he was displeased to note she'd removed the ring.

Tristan's casual posture did nothing to mask his obvious irritation and Mel knew it wasn't lost on the other nine students as they struggled to decide if Professor Everett was serious about his threat. But Mel knew he was 100 percent serious. He'd failed a student in her class at Columbia for missing too many classes. Right now, Mel knew he wasn't thinking about the other students in the class. It was as though they'd ceased to exist. All his attention was focused on her. Mel bit her lip, praying he'd remember where they were and turn back to the class. Having Tristan's undivided attention on her made her antsy. Only an hour earlier he'd held her down on the bed, licking from her neck to her toes. Now, with his jaw clenched, it looked like there was nothing he'd rather do than pull her over his knee and spank her until she begged him to stop.

Mel felt her face turn crimson and Tristan finally turned away, giving Mel a chance to catch her breath.

"Now, if there are no questions, let's begin."

The rest of the class passed in a blur. After Tristan explained his requirements, they went through the syllabus. She knew he wanted to make sure that there was never a moment of confusion between him and the rest of his students. He was in charge. And he expected the most from his students.

After an hour and a half, Tristan finally glanced at his watch. "You can go. I'll see you on Wednesday." He turned to the blackboard before glancing over his shoulder. "Miss Potter, can I have a word?"

His stern tone left no room for discussion and the room went silent. Mel could feel her classmates watching her. Mel glared at Tristan. This wasn't how she was supposed to begin graduate school. Being kept after class like an errant child.

"Of course," Mel responded dryly. In retrospect, maybe she shouldn't have removed the ring, but it was too late now. She tapped her foot impatiently, waiting for everyone to leave. Waiting until she was alone with Tristan.

He turned back to her and she felt that familiar flutter

in her chest, the way she always did when he looked at her. The amazement that still filled her whenever she thought about this man being hers. He looked breathtaking, standing in front of the chalkboard, his casual posture doing nothing to hide the taut muscles that lay beneath his simple yet elegant clothing. He looked perfect. Irresistible.

This was a man in charge. And right now, all his attention was focused on Mel.

"Were you planning on telling me you were going to be my professor?" she asked before Tristan had a chance to speak.

He wasn't the only one who was pissed off. She shouldn't have been caught off guard like that.

He shrugged his broad shoulders and began collecting his things. "Professor Ruiz had a family emergency. They asked me to teach the class two days ago. And we haven't exactly had much time to discuss our schedules," he said, fixing his eyes on Mel.

Mel blushed. No, they certainly hadn't done much talking the past week. Everything happened so fast. The Emile Fellowship. The move to Princeton. The engagement. They'd spent the last week packing up Tristan's belongings from his apartment in New York. And when they weren't packing, they'd been in bed. If she'd thought the sexual dynamic between them would dampen, now that they were truly together, she'd been wrong. If anything, the opposite was true. As their connection deepened, the trust between them growing stronger, their sexual connection was all that more powerful. Just being in the same room as Tristan made Mel's body respond. And after an hour and a half of watching Tristan control a classroom, Mel was wet.

"You should have told me," she added stubbornly.

Tristan froze, his gaze slowly coming up to meet Mel's. "Truthfully, I didn't know until I looked at the roster this morning." He tore his eyes away, shoving the last of his things into his worn leather briefcase. "Walk with me."

He started towards the door, not giving Mel a chance to respond. Grudgingly, Mel followed close behind, thankful that they were the only two in the hallway. Tristan walked quickly, forcing Mel to pick up the pace to keep up with him. He didn't turn and he didn't slow and Mel could tell he was just as out of sorts as she was.

By the time Tristan unlocked his office door, Mel was out of breath. He held the door open and she stepped around him, catching a hint of his masculine cologne as she entered his office.

"Melissa, this might take a while. Would you tell Professor Gaskell I will reschedule with him this afternoon?" Tristan called over his shoulder and Mel felt her heart rate accelerate. She heard the door shut behind her and Tristan flipping the lock.

"I don't think that's a good idea," she said hesitantly. They'd gone over the university policy about students and professors together. Whatever Tristan had in mind definitely defied that policy.

"Melanie," he said in a stern voice that sent a shiver running down her spine, ending at her sex.

Mel turned slowly to find him leaning against the door looking devilishly handsome. Not that Tristan Everett ever looked anything less. There was a slight wash of dark stubble along his strong jaw and his hands were shoved into the pockets of his navy chinos. He looked every bit the part of seductive professor and Mel swallowed hard when she saw his jaw twitch.

"What?"

"I think you forgot something when you left the house this morning," he said slowly.

Mel shook her head. "No, I'm fairly certain I didn't forget a thing."

"Think harder."

Mel pretended to think before shaking her head, feeling her hair come loose around her shoulders. "No, I think I remembered everything." Mel knew she was playing a dangerous game and yet she couldn't seem to stop herself.

Tristan pushed off the wall, stalking slowly towards her and Mel found herself backing up until she hit the desk. Trapped, she crossed her arms over her chest. Tristan towered over her, his posture unyielding and she felt her sex tingle. Mel bit her lip, trying to hide how aroused this made her. Everything about Tristan turned her on. But especially this side of him.

Tristan cocked his head to the side. "Do you really want to play this game with me?"

Mel's body begged for Tristan's touch, to feel his hands raking through her hair as he crushed her body against his, but he didn't move. Instead, he watched her, maintaining the infuriating distance between them. She could smell him, the scent simultaneously arousing and comforting.

"When I left this morning, I distinctly remember you wearing my ring." Tristan's eyes fixed on her hand, clutching the desk behind her. "Don't tell me you're having second thoughts." Tristan lifted one eyebrow as he watched Mel intently.

Mel swallowed hard before letting out a ragged laugh. "Second thoughts? Are you fucking kidding me?"

Something about the way Tristan shrugged his shoulders, that studied nonchalance, made Mel suddenly worry that he'd actually spent the last two hours thinking she'd changed her mind.

"Tristan, I love you. No doubts. No worries. I. Love. You."

She saw a flicker of relief in his dark eyes. Then, just as quickly it was gone. And Tristan pulled himself up to his full imposing height.

"In that case," Tristan said slowly, "there'd better be a damn good reason why that ring isn't on your finger."

Mel gulped. "I remember you saying something about not wanting to draw attention to us until we told the administration. And that ring, though lovely, isn't exactly subtle." It was true. The large, emerald cut diamond ring Tristan had given her was anything but subtle. It was absolutely stunning, and when he'd told her it had belonged to his mother, she'd been overwhelmed. Not just by its beauty, but by its obvious importance to him. This wasn't just any ring. And she'd taken it off, shoving it carelessly into her purse.

"Tristan…" she started to apologize but he shook his head, not letting her finish.

"Mel, it fucking kills me that I can't tell the entire world that you're mine." He ran his hand through his hair in frustration. "That I can't take your hand when we're together. I fucking hate it." Tristan sighed, his voice softening slightly when he added, "You didn't see how those boys in class looked at you."

Mel's eyes went wide and she let out a laugh. "You're afraid someone is going to hit on me?"

Tristan gave her a bashful shrug.

Mel felt her heart swell and she reached out, letting her fingers flutter along Tristan's jaw. "Who cares about them? Tristan, you're the only man for me. Being in that classroom with you, I didn't notice anyone else. I could barely pay attention to what you were saying. It's you. Only you."

Tristan glowered, but she could feel him softening gradually, the tension leaving his body.

"Put it on."

Mel smiled, running her thumb across his lower lip and Tristan sucked her finger into his mouth, suckling her and she felt her nipples harden.

"I should take you over my knee, but I suspect you'd enjoy that too much," he added. Mel only smiled in response, knowing that he was right. She loved when he spanked her. Just thinking about it made her hot and ready and she looked around the spacious office. It wouldn't be the first time that Tristan took her over his knee in his office.

She took the ring out of her bag and Tristan gingerly took it from her, sliding it onto her finger. He cradled her hand in his, admiring it before bringing it to his lips and kissing her palm.

"I'm serious, Mel. I don't want you taking this off."

Mel found herself nodding. They'd figure out what to tell people. But for now, she only wanted to reassure the man standing in front of her. The man who in such a short period of time had come to be her entire world. She hated seeing him like this. Vulnerable. Aching. Couldn't he see how much he meant to her?

She opened her eyes wide, letting her lips part provocatively. "Is there anything I can do to reassure you,

Professor Everett?" she asked breathily and she saw a flicker of interest in Tristan's dark eyes. Without breaking eye contact, Mel reached down, running her hand over Tristan's growing hardness and she watched his eyes close as a moan of pleasure escaped his lips. She loved that she could do this to him. That her touch was enough to make him lose it.

"You were very generous this morning, Professor Everett. Let me return the favor," she said, pushing him back before dropping to her knees. She kept her eyes on his face as she pulled down his zipper, freeing his magnificent erection. Mel licked her lips. Just seeing him, erect, straining, made her sex slippery with need and she couldn't wait to feel him inside her, stretching her, pushing her to the edge. Her tongue darted from her mouth, flicking across his head, tasting him, and Tristan moaned again, his hands finding her hair and holding her fast.

She opened her lips wide and sucked him into her wet mouth, feeling him twitch against her tongue and Mel couldn't help the wash of pride that filled her as she sucked him deeper.

"Mel," he groaned and when she looked up, she saw the look of pure adoration in his eyes. She wanted to feel him come apart, wanted to feel him lose control, wanted to comfort him with her body and her touch. There were times when words weren't enough to convey what she felt for him.

His fingers dug into her scalp as she relaxed her throat, taking him all the way until his coarse hairs tickled her nose and all she could do was relax as he fucked her mouth.

She wanted to taste him. Wanted to drink him up.

His eyes closed as his movements grew more frantic, more demanding and she dug her fingers into his ass, pulling him deeper, sucking him harder.

Surprise washed over her when his hands found her shoulders, pushing her away gently. When she looked up, Tristan was sucking in a shallow breath, his eyes wide and unfocused.

"Mel, no," he said firmly.

She frowned. "Why not?"

He shook his head. "I don't want to come in your mouth." He grabbed Mel's hand, pulling her to her feet. "You're going to be very, very quiet," he whispered into her ear and Mel felt a shiver of excitement as she took one last look over at the door.

"Get on the desk."

Mel didn't need to be told twice. She hoisted herself up and let her legs fall open. Tristan pushed up her skirt roughly and Mel could see the hunger clear in his eyes as he shook his head disapprovingly. "It seems you forgot something else when you left the house earlier," he said, his eyes noting the underwear that Mel was wearing.

"How was I supposed to know I'd get called into your office this morning?" she teased. Tristan ran one finger along her sex, feeling how wet and ready she was through the damp cotton of her panties. He groaned, pushing them aside and sinking his finger in to the hilt. Mel squeezed down on him, trying to draw him deeper.

"I'm all for foreplay, but right now I need you inside me," Mel said, eliciting a growl from Tristan.

He yanked down her panties and she could feel his eyes feasting on her exposed sex. He grinned before grabbing Mel's hips and burying himself into her with a single thrust. Mel shuddered around him, her head falling back as she struggled to accommodate him. He felt perfect. He felt like home.

Tristan wrapped his arms around her, pulling her fast against his chest as he fucked her roughly, his breathing erratic and Mel bit her lip, willing herself not to make a sound as a delicious feeling began at her toes and spread through her.

"Are you close?" Tristan rasped and Mel nodded, unable to find the words to respond.

"Good, because I'm not going to last. I've wanted to fuck you since you stepped into my classroom this morning." Tristan pumped into her and Mel met his powerful thrusts with her own, lifting her hips in time with his until she felt him come inside her, filling her with his hot release as her body quivered beneath him, her mouth gaping in a silent cry of pleasure.

Tristan pulled out, feeling a twinge of guilt. He'd only wanted to talk to Mel, but the moment she dropped to her knees, he'd been powerless before her. He ran one hand through his hair distractedly, glancing at the door.

Closed-door meetings with students weren't exactly the norm and he was suddenly concerned someone might have heard them. The last thing he needed this week was for someone to think he was having an affair with one of his students. Tristan had an impeccable reputation as a professional. And he had no intention of destroying all he'd worked on now.

Not that this was an affair. This was Mel. His Mel. And sometimes when he was with her, he couldn't think rationally. He just needed her.

When he turned back to Mel, she was sitting in the same position on his desk, her legs spread wide and he could see his come spilling from her sex. She blinked, as if taken by surprise. Her cheeks were tinged pink and her lips parted and wet. Jesus. He shook his head, letting his eyes return to her beautiful cunt. He couldn't think of a sexier image in the world.

There was no way Mel could stay in his class. It would be pure torture. How could he be expected to teach when she kept looking at him like that with her big green eyes?

He shook his head again. "Let me get you a tissue," he muttered, suddenly coming to his senses.

"Don't bother. I like it," Mel said, pulling her panties up and giving him the sweetest smile. "I love feeling you inside me."

He groaned. Sometimes, he wondered if she had any idea of the affect her words had on him. Just hearing those words come from her perfect, innocent looking mouth, knowing she loved this just as much as he did was enough to drive him crazy.

He grabbed her hand, once again feeling a wave of satisfaction at seeing his ring on her finger, knowing that she was his. He brought her delicate palm to his lips and kissed it.

"I love you." When he looked up, he saw the pleasure in her bright green eyes.

"I love you, too," she whispered back.

Tristan could feel those three words to his very center and he still couldn't believe what they did to him. He grinned, pulling Mel into his chest, unable to resist the urge to hold her for a moment. To feel her supple body against his. She buried her nose into his chest, inhaling deeply.

She was perfect.

He cupped her chin in his hands, bringing her lips to his. "I have a meeting this evening but I'll see you at home after?"

The smile that Mel gave him made his knees weak and it took all his will to release her. He wanted to hold her like this forever. Wanted her always in his arms.

It was a disorienting feeling. This need he couldn't control. And yet, he wouldn't change it for the world.

He gave her a swat on her ass, trying to regain his composure. "Get out of here, I have work to do." He could feel the silly grin on his face.

He knew Mel was teasing him with the way she swung her hips provocatively as she made her way to the door. She opened the door before turning around and giving him a playful smile. She was practically glowing and he knew his seed was pouring from her pussy, marking her as his.

"Thanks for meeting with me, Professor Everett," she said sweetly before stepping into the outer office.

CHAPTER TWO

"Have you given any thought to the wedding?" Tristan asked, coming to stand behind Mel and putting his large hands on her hips, drawing her closer.

"Seriously? It's been a week." Mel laughed, but she knew Tristan was completely serious.

Mel felt Tristan nuzzle into her neck and she tilted her head to the side, granting him more access. He nipped her skin softly, making her moan in response. She loved when he kissed her neck, the feeling both intimate and erotic.

"Don't make me wait," he groaned, grinding Mel's hips into his and she could feel his erection digging insistently into her back.

"I just started school!" Mel protested, knowing it was useless. From the second she said yes in New York, Tristan had been asking her when she wanted to get married. It wasn't that she wanted to wait, but everything was moving so fast. She'd never thought she'd get married so young. She thought there would be more time. To settle into school. To focus on her career. But Tristan was a whirlwind, impossible to ignore. Not that she'd want to. Here, in his arms, was exactly how she wanted to spend the rest of her life. Still, between moving and getting ready for classes to start, she hadn't had time to think.

"Have you called your parents?"

Mel stiffened. "Not yet."

"You have to call them."

"Can't it just be the two of us, just for a little, before everyone finds out?"

Tristan dug his fingers into Mel's hips, and Mel could feel his hot breath on her neck, his powerful presence enough to set her skin on fire.

"What if I want the whole world to find out?" he responded petulantly, making Mel laugh and almost forget what was at stake. Tristan didn't know anything about her parents except that they lived on Long Island. That was all he'd needed to know.

Except now, he wanted to meet them. And no matter how much Mel knew he had every right to ask that, she couldn't help but feel harassed by the request.

It would be putting it mildly to say that Mel and her parents didn't exactly see eye-to-eye. They hadn't spoken since she'd informed them she was going to graduate school in Comparative Literature. It didn't matter that it was at an Ivy League university, it was never enough. Her father had looked at her and asked contemptuously what she planned on doing with a PhD in literature. When she'd told him that she wanted to teach, he'd scoffed. "Potters don't teach."

That was six months ago, but the words still stung as though it were last week.

"Just a little time? Please?" Mel begged, rolling her hips.

She knew it was wrong to use sex, but maybe if she distracted him, he'd forget.

Tristan slipped a hand beneath Mel's skirt, his fingers brushing over her sensitive sex, making Mel moan. She knew he could feel her arousal seeping through the fabric, making it slick and slippery. She was so ready for him. She always was. All he had to do was kiss her.

Tristan's fingers eased the fabric aside and he slid one finger up and down her slick sex, sending an electric current through Mel's entire body. Her nipples peaked and her lips fell open as she ground back into him.

"You're aroused," Tristan stated matter-of-factly. Mel couldn't deny it even if she wanted to. Tristan spread her lips, letting the cool air bathe her sex, making her squirm impatiently. "Should I fuck you?" Tristan teased and Mel nodded frantically.

"Don't make me beg."

Tristan chuckled, throwing Mel off balance. Suddenly she worried if Tristan was the one in control, the one holding the reigns while Mel stood helpless before him.

"Call your parents," he whispered.

"I will, I promise."

"Not good enough." He sucked her earlobe into his mouth, his teeth grazing the plump flesh, making Mel gasp in surprise.

Fuck, fuck, fuck, Mel thought, rubbing her ass against Tristan's growing erection. She wanted him. She wanted him so bad it practically hurt. It didn't matter how many times she had him, she always wanted more. And she wasn't the only one who knew that.

"Not going to work," he admonished sternly, his fingers continuing to toy with her sex, carefully skirting her clit, making Mel moan out in frustration.

"I'll call them, I swear," Mel moaned as Tristan teased her opening, his finger dipping in slightly before withdrawing and Mel tilted her hips, trying to take him deeper.

When his thumb brushed her clit, just for a second, Mel jumped, but Tristan kept one hand fiercely on her hip, locking her in place.

"I'm serious, Mel. Call them. They need to know I intend on marrying you. And I'm running out of patience."

Somewhere in her lust-fogged brain, Mel could hear the need in his voice. Not a sexual need, but something else. Like he was afraid that she wouldn't tell them. Like he was afraid that until she did, none of this would be real.

Mel wrapped her hand around Tristan's, pressing it harder into her sex as she wiggled back against him.

"I'll call them."

He slid a finger into her sex and Mel let her eyes flutter closed, trying to lose herself in the sensation. Of Tristan, filling her. Of Tristan, having his way with her.

"If you don't call them, there will be consequences."

Just the way he said consequences sent a shiver of excitement through Mel, and her already hard nipples throbbed painfully, begging for his touch, begging for his lips.

"Consequences. Got it," she panted. "Will you please fuck me now?" Her voice was reedy but Mel was too lost in the moment.

"Should I make you come? Is that what you want?"

He slid another finger into Mel's sex and her whole body tightened around him.

"I'll take that as a yes," he said, chuckling. Mel cried

out, suddenly bereft of his fingers, and then he was spinning her around, his lips crashing down on hers, taking her mouth with a fierce desire that made Mel's entire body sag with relief.

CHAPTER THREE

The rest of the week went smoothly after the initial surprise of finding Tristan in her classroom. So far, everyone in her cohort seemed nice and intelligent and Mel was nervously looking forward to tonight's cocktail hour. Every year, Dean Hannum hosted all the students and faculty at his home for a chance to get to know each other better. Mel would have been nervous even without Tristan being there, but somehow, she didn't know how she'd be able to get through the night pretending Tristan was just another faculty member.

"Are you going tonight?"

Tristan looked up from the book he was reading, his head tilting as he considered her. "Of course."

"We need to tell them, don't we?" Mel asked, coming to sit on the arm of the sofa. She didn't want to tell the Department. She didn't want to be known as the graduate student sleeping with the professor. Engaged to her professor, she silently corrected herself. Somehow, that distinction didn't make it any easier to swallow. She knew her classmates would look at her differently once they found out. That they would judge her. Because if she were truly being honest, wouldn't Mel have the same reaction?

To them, she'd be that girl. The one naïve enough to fall for a professor. They'd pity her, just waiting for the other shoe to drop. For Tristan to find someone new, someone younger. Because they'd assume she was being taken advantage of. That the older professor was just getting his fill of her before he discarded her and moved on to the next, younger student.

Mel frowned. She hated that they'd think of Tristan like that. That they wouldn't be able to see past their prejudices to see the way he looked at her, the way he watched her, the love in his eyes. But there was no way to explain that to the other people in the program.

And the only thing worse than seeing that condescending pity in their eyes would be knowing they thought she was gaining favors because of her relationship with him. They couldn't be more wrong. If anything, he'd expect more of her, would push her harder.

"What do you think they're going to say?" she asked softly.

Tristan's lips came together in thought and Mel had to resist the urge to run her finger over them. He had such beautiful, expressive lips.

"I assume they'll be less than pleased, but there isn't much they can do about it. Likely, we will have to come to some agreement about the grading of your papers, because I won't be allowed to grade them myself."

"Why not?"

Tristan gave her a look that said are you really this naïve and she just shrugged her shoulders.

"Objectivity. There is no way that I could be objective, reading your work. And they will know that. Most likely, someone else will review your work."

"Who?"

Tristan shrugged. "We'll just have to wait to find out."

"I could always drop the class."

"Absolutely not."

"Why? I can always take it another semester. And I don't think either of us will be able to concentrate if I'm there."

Tristan frowned but didn't respond and Mel knew she was right. There wasn't any way that they'd be able to focus. As much as she loved watching Tristan teach, dropping the class was the best option and they both knew it.

Tristan put his book on the couch. "Have you decided what you're wearing tonight?" Tristan asked, abruptly changing the subject.

Mel's eyes narrowed. "No. Why?"

Tristan gave her an innocent smile that Mel knew was anything but innocent. "I bought you something."

Mel rolled her eyes. "Of course you did."

"I think you're going to really like it."

"Am I?"

"Yes," he purred, coming to his feet and leaning down, kissing Mel. "You are definitely going to like it," he said, stepping back. Mel pouted. She didn't know how he could still do that. One kiss and she was a goner. She brushed her hair out of her face.

When she reached out, Tristan sidestepped her with a playful laugh and walked out of the room, leaving Mel to stare after him in frustration.

Sometimes it seemed like he really was trying to torture her.

She had to smile. Because she knew he felt the exact same way about her.

Tristan returned with a black gift bag and handed it to her, watching her intently as she opened it. Inside was a small black box and she took it out, giving Tristan a questioning look.

"Open it."

He didn't have to tell her twice. Mel placed the lid aside and found herself staring at two black orbs. She looked up, the question evident on her face.

"What are these?"

"Love beads," he said, reaching over Mel's shoulder and lifting one of the beads in his hand. Mel watched it roll around on his palm. "You're going to put them inside of you and wear them at the cocktail party tonight. I may not be able to touch you while we're there, but you certainly won't forget me this way."

Mel laughed nervously. "How could I ever forget you?" she whispered. He had to know she thought about him constantly, that he was a part of her now that she'd never be able to escape.

"Get on the couch and put your ass in the air. I want to put these in you myself."

Mel felt the hairs on the back of her neck prickle with excitement as she scurried to get into position. Tristan lifted the skirt of her dress, exposing her ass to him and she wiggled her hips, suddenly self-conscious.

Not that she had anything to worry about. Tristan had seen every inch of her body. Sometimes it felt like he knew her better than she knew herself.

Gingerly, he pulled down her underwear and pressed his lips firmly against the swell of her ass, the gesture sweet and calming and Mel felt herself relaxing.

"I want you thinking about me all night. Every time one of those silly boys flirts with you, remember me. Remember how I'm going to fuck you when we get home at the end of the night. Remember it's my name you'll be screaming when I finally let you come."

Mel felt her sex grow slick at the promise in his words, her pussy pulsing with a need she knew would go unsatisfied until later.

Mel shivered as Tristan's breath moved lower. His strong hands spread her ass, exposing every inch of her to him. Mel squirmed as his tongue ran down her cleft, his lips pausing over her puckered entrance. Mel's entire body tensed.

"Relax."

Tristan's insistent tongue pressed into her, making her squirm. It felt so wrong. Wrong and yet, at the same time, Mel couldn't deny the affect it was having on her.

She felt him penetrating her in shallow thrusts and Mel arched her back, letting him.

Suddenly, his tongue was moving lower, lapping at her dripping sex.

"I'm looking forward to fucking that beautiful ass of yours while your tight cunt clutches these balls. I think you'll find it a very, very enjoyable experience."

Mel shuddered as Tristan slid the first ball into her slippery sex, finding no resistance. He brushed her clit once, making her start, before sliding in the second ball. Mel wiggled her hips, feeling the weighted balls move inside her, forcing her pussy to clench around them, anchoring them deep inside of her.

He wanted her to keep these in all night?

Mel bit her lip. She couldn't tell if she was excited or terrified.

Tristan gave her ass a firm slap, the sound echoing through the apartment and Mel felt the tingly warmth spread across her skin as the beads shifted, sending an erotic thrill through her.

She sucked in a ragged breath. Tonight was definitely going to be interesting, she thought wryly.

CHAPTER FOUR

Mel looked stunning. The black cocktail dress she'd elected to wear highlighted her porcelain skin and she'd gathered her auburn locks into a loose bun at the nape of her neck.

Tristan couldn't help but notice the slight flush of her cheeks and the way her lips remained parted.

To anyone else, it would look like the affect of a couple of glasses of wine, but Tristan knew better. Every time she moved, the love beads shifted inside her and she had to clamp down to guarantee they didn't slip out.

Maybe it was cruel of him, but he'd insisted she not wear any panties.

She stood near the stairway, her back to the wall, talking to a pretty blonde student, but next to Mel, the other woman looked ordinary. Hell, next to Mel, everyone was ordinary. She glowed. And it wasn't just with arousal. That was just Mel. It still seemed amazing to him that she was oblivious to the affect she had on others. Of the way every man in the room had noticed her arrival.

Tristan scowled, turning back to Professor Gaskell. He was a fixture in the Comparative Lit Department and exactly the type of professor Tristan detested. Stolid. Complacent. He'd lost the spark that made some professors great and all that remained was a comfortable man with an obvious fondness for younger women and spirits.

Tristan had seen the way he looked at Mel when she walked in and he'd simply clenched his fists, trying to ignore the obvious interest she'd aroused.

"What were you saying?" Tristan asked, trying to focus on the man in front of him instead of the beautiful woman across the room. There'd be more than enough time later to focus his attention on Mel.

"How are you settling in?"

Tristan found himself smiling and he brought his whiskey to his lips, savoring the burn as it slid down his throat. "Quite well, I'd say."

"You don't miss the city?"

Tristan gave him a tight smile. "No, I've managed to find enough to excite me here." Nothing in New York could compete with the joy of being in the same room as Mel.

Professor Gaskell nodded, finishing off the last of his drink. "Want another?"

Tristan shook his head. If he had much more to drink, he'd be liable to do something profoundly reckless. Like drag Mel up to the second floor bathroom, fucking her hard and fast, relieving the need that had been building steadily throughout the night.

Tristan glanced around the sumptuous living room, wondering if there was anyone else he needed to talk to before the night was over. He'd met most of the faculty at the Department meeting before classes started. The students were a different story. As he looked around the room, he recognized few, but he knew that they would approach him if they wanted.

Tristan took another sip of his whiskey, rolling it around on his tongue. Out of the corner of his eye, he noticed Mel talking to one of the other first years from his Postmodernism class. Tristan frowned and turned away, his jaw clenching.

He'd have to be blind not to notice the way the other men in the room looked at Mel. They'd arrived separately, knowing it wouldn't have looked right if they'd come together. And even though he hadn't spoken to her since she'd gotten there, he was keenly aware of her presence.

And while he might not be able to go over there and put his arm around her waist, making it clear to everyone else that she was his, at least she was wearing his ring. He'd seen it sparkling in the low light, filling him with satisfaction. He may have been the only person there who knew she was his, but that didn't matter. He just hoped the other students weren't too young to notice an engagement ring. At their age, Tristan hadn't yet learned to look at a woman's hands before approaching her.

Tristan let out of a sigh. Every moment they had to pretend to be casual acquaintances was pure agony. And yet, Tristan was reluctant to take that next step, knowing full well the impact it would have on both of them. Whatever the university did to him, Tristan could handle it. He worried about Mel. About the impact their relationship would have on her. It was a competitive program and he knew just how cruel people could be when they saw something they perceived as a weakness.

"And you must be *the* Tristan Everett," a lilting voice caught his attention and Tristan looked up sharply from his drink, concentrating on smoothing his frown. Standing in front of him was a woman around his age. Mid-thirties with tortoise shell glasses sliding down her nose that did nothing to mask her exotic beauty. Long dark waves hung over one shoulder, giving the impression of a woman who'd just slipped out of bed, leaving a very satisfied lover behind.

At a different time in his life, Tristan would have been drawn to her, but now, he was merely thankful for the distraction.

"That depends on what you've heard," he said, tilting his head, trying to place her. She looked vaguely familiar.

She reached out a manicured hand. "Isabella Ferreiro," she said with a smile and he recognized her name instantly. She was the Portuguese lecturer Gaskell had been talking about earlier.

A thin sheen of perspiration clung to Mel's skin. At first, she'd thought the love beads wouldn't be a problem, their subtle vibrations easy enough to ignore, but as the night wore on, every movement sent a jolt of awareness through her body. Her pussy clenched the beads, desperately holding them in place.

More than once, she'd panicked, afraid they'd slip free.

She couldn't imagine anything more humiliating.

She was going to kill Tristan.

How the hell was she supposed to make pleasant conversation when all she could think about was escaping to the bathroom to give herself the release she so desperately craved?

She'd seen the twitch of a smile on Tristan's lips when she'd walked in, flustered and agitated. He knew exactly what she was feeling. Mel brushed her hair from her face and took a sip of wine, praying it would help relieve some of the pressure she was feeling.

So far, it wasn't working.

"You're in my Postmodernism class."

Mel nearly jumped and it took her a moment before she was able to collect herself enough to smile at the man standing in front of her. He extended his hand. "Tom Walker. How's your night so far?" he asked, looking around the room before smiling back at Mel.

"You have no idea."

"Here, I got you a refill. You looked like you needed one."

Mel thankfully took the glass of wine he held out to her, taking a long sip of it.

"Anything I can do to help?"

"Excuse me?"

"With whatever's bothering you."

Mel wanted to laugh. The only thing that could help her now was to get these damned things out of her. And since that wasn't about to happen, she just shook her head. "I've had a long week."

He laughed, his voice warm and friendly. He looked like a football player. Athletic and blond. "Does it have anything to do with Everett? You two didn't seem to hit it off the first day of class."

If only you knew, Mel thought. "No, we talked after class. Everything is fine."

Tom gave her an incredulous look and Mel just

shrugged and added, "We knew each other from Columbia. I didn't realize he was teaching the class, otherwise I would have made sure to be on time. Professor Everett has a thing about tardiness." As soon as the words were out of her mouth, Mel regretted them. "I'm going to grab something to eat. Do you want anything?"

Tom rolled his shoulders. "I'll come with. I'm starved."

With every step, Mel felt her anxiety heightening. She couldn't escape the sensual sensations coursing through her and she hoped to God no one would notice. Still, she couldn't deny the fact that being in public, not wearing underwear, with the love beads in her was turning her on. It wasn't just the physical sensations they caused. It was knowing that she was doing something so wrong and that this room full of people had no idea.

She glanced across the room to where she'd last seen Tristan, wanting to glare at him for putting her through his, and found him talking to a beautiful brunette. She frowned. The woman had her hand resting on Tristan's shoulder and Mel stumbled and suddenly Tom's arm was around her waist, steadying her. Just that simple touch set her skin on fire and she pushed him off hastily.

Even the slightest touch was enough to make everything she felt heightened.

"Sorry, I think I've probably had a little too much to drink," she mumbled, trying her best to laugh it off.

Tom grinned, showing off his perfect white teeth. "Nothing to be sorry about. I'm well on my way as well."

Mel felt Tristan's eyes boring into her and she straightened up. "Then why don't you grab us another round while I get some food."

He flashed her a toothy grin. "I knew I was going to

like you."

Inside, Mel grimaced but she kept the smile on her face. She needed to go to the bathroom and take out these damned beads before she went insane. Too bad Tristan would probably object.

She glared at him across the room, oblivious to the people circling around her, their voices growing louder and more insistent as the evening wore on. She grabbed her phone from her purse, angrily punching the keys. *You are a cruel man.*

She slipped her phone back in her purse and marveled at the table of food in front of her. At least the Comparative Literature Department had gone all out. There were finger sandwiches, cured meats, cheeses, a plate overflowing with fruit. Mel took a small paper plate and loaded it up, trying her best to limit the movements of her body.

She felt like she was going to combust. Every step she took sent a thrill to her core that was unavoidable. She bit her lip in frustration. If she could just go to the bathroom for a few minutes...

She shook her head. No way could she leave the cocktail mixer to do what she was thinking. No matter how tempting the idea might be.

And it was definitely tempting.

Instead, she took a bite of a roast beef sandwich, letting out a little sigh of pleasure. Thank God for food at a time like this.

"Here." Tom handed her another glass of wine. Mel couldn't remember how many of these little plastic cups she'd had so far, but she didn't care. She'd have a hangover in the morning, but luckily, she didn't have any classes on

Friday. She could spend the entire day in bed if that's what she wanted.

Mel's phone vibrated, making her jump. She glanced at the screen and blanched. *Don't even think about taking them out.*

She bit the corner of her lip. It was like he could read her mind, which only made the way he was toying with her all that much more cruel.

"Everything okay?" Tom asked good-naturedly.

"Yeah, everything's fine," she mumbled.

"So, how are you liking school so far?" Tom asked, his bright blue eyes flashing.

Mel scrunched up her nose. "It's a little overwhelming, actually." As she said it, Mel realized it wasn't school that was overwhelming, it was Tristan.

"Some of us are getting together for a barbecue at my apartment this weekend. You know, get to know everyone and all that. I'm feeling a little lost myself. You should come."

"Where are you from?"

"Boston. But I've been in San Francisco the past few years. I know it's only been a few weeks, but I miss it."

Mel laughed. "I understand."

"What about you?"

"New York, but I've been down here all summer working for Professor Taylor."

"Does it get better?"

Mel laughed, but before she had a chance to respond, a smooth, familiar voice interrupted, causing goose bumps to break out across her skin. "Ms. Potter, Mr. Walker, how are you both tonight?"

Mel could practically feel Tristan standing behind her,

the energy and power that radiated off him, making her whole body perk to attention.

She turned slowly, feeling his eyes trail over her face before he turned expectantly to Tom.

Tom laughed. "Still getting the hang of everything, I suppose."

Tristan gave him a curt nod and Mel wondered if he was jealous that she'd been talking to Tom.

"Having another glass of wine and then calling it a night," Mel said.

Tristan made a show of checking his wristwatch and Mel found herself holding her breath as she waited for his response. "So early?"

"I've had a grueling day."

"Really?"

Mel could see the playful twinkle in Tristan's eye and she gritted her teeth before responding tersely, "Really."

Tristan cocked his head and Mel could tell he was loving every second of this.

"Do you mind if I grab Ms. Potter from you for a moment? There's someone I promised to introduce her to."

Tom just shrugged his broad shoulders.

Tristan didn't have to touch her for Mel to feel his presence on her body as they walked across the room.

"Tell me, are you attracted to young Mr. Walker?" he murmured in a low voice that only Mel could hear. She stopped abruptly and turned.

"Terribly. I practically dragged him out of the room just to let him have his way with me," she said, her face completely devoid of emotion.

Tristan was still for a moment and then the corners of

his lips turned up in amusement.

"Someone's testy," he teased and it took all of Mel's willpower not to shove him.

"Someone has put me in a rather uncomfortable position," Mel responded dryly. "So who did you want to introduce me to? Because if you don't let me leave soon, I'm not going to be held responsible for my actions."

"And what would you do?" Tristan asked, his curiosity piqued.

"I do remember seeing a bathroom at the top of the stairs."

"You wouldn't."

Mel fixed her eyes on Tristan. "I guess you'll never know."

Tristan kicked the door shut behind him and spun Mel around.

"You have no idea what a torture tonight has been," he growled into her neck and Mel arched her back, feeling his hot breath on her already flushed skin.

"Trust me, I have a pretty good idea."

Tristan chuckled. "Get on the couch. And don't bother getting undressed."

Mel sat down, breathing heavily, parting her legs and pulling her skirt up. For a long moment, Tristan just stared at her, his eyes wild. He licked his lips slowly, and Mel swore she could feel his tongue on her skin, tasting her. And then he was on her, pushing her legs apart, his face dipping between her thighs, licking along her seam. Mel moaned, lifting her hips from the couch to meet him.

It felt divine. She squeezed down on the love beads, feeling them move inside her, sending all new sensations through her.

"Oh fuck, don't stop," she groaned, squeezing her eyes shut.

Tristan glanced up, his tongue poised over her clit. "Keep your eyes on me. I'm going to make you come and then I'm going to fuck that delicious ass of yours."

Mel swallowed hard but managed to nod her head. His words sent a rush of excitement through her. She'd never wanted to have anal sex before, but right now, she didn't care what Tristan did, just as long as he made her come first.

"That's my girl," he murmured into her sex, his eyes staying locked on hers as he once again lowered his tongue, flicking it against her clit, making Mel scream out. He reached beneath her, gripping her ass in his hands, holding her open and immobilized.

"I want to hear you scream," he murmured, burying his head between her thighs and Mel could feel his fingers reaching behind her, brushing against her ass, making her go wild.

This man was dangerous. Mel ran her hands through his wild, tousled hair, catching a glimpse of her diamond ring as it reflected in the low light. Dangerous and all hers. She smiled and it was all she could do not to come apart on the spot.

Just as Mel felt the first stirrings of her powerful orgasm, Tristan yanked on the cord attached to the balls inside her and it was like an electric current traveling down her spine and Mel let out a scream, unable to contain herself as Tristan continued feasting on her sex.

CHAPTER FIVE

"Mine," Tristan whispered. He could hear the desperation in his voice as he gathered Mel's trembling body against his chest and he couldn't tell if he was talking to himself or to the breathtaking woman in his arms. It was ridiculous, but seeing Mel with Tom Walker earlier had made him wild with jealousy. Knowing that publicly they had to keep up this bullshit charade made him want to storm into Dean Hannum's office and tell him the truth. That Mel was his.

Tristan carried Mel's spent body into the bedroom, gingerly resting her on the bed. How many times had he imagined this moment? And yet, he still couldn't believe Mel was willing to give him this last piece of herself.

Mel stretched her arms above her head, watching him with wide, unfocused eyes. She looked soft, contented, and yet, he knew a fire burned beneath.

They were made for each other, he thought, tossing aside his shirt and unbuckling his belt. No one had ever made him want so acutely. This insatiable need he was helpless to fight. He needed Mel like he needed air to breathe. He could feel it, threatening to overtake him, threatening to erase all else until they were all that remained, their bodies fused together.

Tristan's throbbing erection sprang free and he watched Mel's eyes light up. When she licked her lower lip, it was like a lightening bolt to his groin. God, she was the sexiest woman on earth and she didn't even know it. Couldn't see the way people responded to her. But Tristan could. And the fact that she'd chosen him, above everyone else, satisfied something deep within him.

"Turn around."

Mel pouted, her eyes caressing his hard cock before she did as he obliged. With one quick movement, he pulled her hair free of its low bun, watching it cascade across her shoulders as its perfume filled the air. Slowly, he eased down the zipper of her dress, exposing inch after inch of beautiful porcelain skin to his hungry gaze. He had to go slow. Had to watch himself. This was Mel's first time. And once he was inside her, he'd be lost, unable to hold back.

Just the idea of burying his hard cock in Mel's tight ass made him throb with impatience. He hadn't realized just how much he needed this until now. Need this final submission and Mel's complete, unwavering trust.

"I want this to be good for you," he said gruffly, turning Mel to face him.

"I know." The sweet smile she gave him stole his breath away and he leaned in, giving her a long, wet kiss, feeling Mel's body soften beneath him.

Grudgingly, he broke away and went to the dresser, returning with a length of black silk and a bottle of lube as Mel discarded her dress. She knelt on the bed, totally naked, her legs parted in invitation and he could see the moisture glistening on her sex. Soon, he thought, his throat choking up with some unknown emotion. Soon every inch of her would be his. His to fuck. But also to love and to cherish. Maybe this was too much, but he wanted her immobilized. Wanted her to give herself over completely to every new sensation. Wanted her struggle and ultimately, her surrender.

"You're going to tie me up." It wasn't a question and Tristan could see the nervous heat in her expressive green eyes as the realization set in. That faint glimmer of fear making his cock swell impatiently.

He liked her like this. No, he fucking loved her like this. Wet. Hot. Uncertain of what was to come but desperate for it anyway. He loved the way her face told him everything she was feeling even when her lips remained sealed.

"Turn around."

Tristan pressed his palm firmly between her shoulder blades, pinning her to the mattress. He drew her arms together, stroking her delicate wrists before binding her hands together and stretching them above her head, securing them to the headboard. In this position, she'd be able to move, but just barely.

"You have no idea what you do to me. Watching you tonight, knowing I couldn't touch you…" Tristan sucked in a deep breath, trying to collect his thoughts. "It nearly broke me. Seeing how hot you were, how your body craved me. Craved the release only I could give you. Mel, you have no idea how perfect you are," Tristan breathed out.

There was nothing sexier than a beautiful, bound

woman. The black silk against her porcelain skin. Her shallow inhalations making her body quake. Her ass lifted and presented to him. She was flawless. And she was his. His to tease and torment. His to love.

"I've wanted to fuck this perfect ass since I came home to find you naked and waiting for me. You should have seen the expression on your face. It was fucking stunning. The way you submitted to me. The way you opened yourself for me. I want every part of you. Every fucking inch of you."

Mel shivered as he ran a finger down her spine, lifting her ass for him without even realizing.

His jaw twitched. He took a deep, steadying breath, assuring himself he was ready before sinking to his knees behind her, trailing kisses along her low back. With every moan from her lips, he felt his dick grow harder. Fuck, he couldn't wait to bury himself in her ass but he knew he had to be careful. Otherwise he'd hurt her. And he'd never, in a million years, be able to forgive himself for hurting her.

"I love knowing I'll be your first and your last," he bit out. With that, he sank a finger into Mel's sex, feeling her quiver around him, her body still on edge from her earlier orgasm. It wouldn't take much to make her come again, he knew, but he wanted her to come when he was inside her. Wanted to feel her tight body milking him to his finish.

He pressed his lips to her ass. "Relax for me, baby," he whispered, his large hands spreading the pale globes of her ass, exposing her last hole to him. With growing impatience, he delved into her pussy, spreading her sweet wetness. God, she was so wet he almost wouldn't need the lube after all.

Watching the black silk go taut as Mel pulled against it, Tristan realized just how good an idea it was to have her restrained. Nothing would be sexier than watching Mel struggle against her bonds as she came apart, screaming his name.

Mel froze when Tristan's tongue brushed against her tight opening. He was the only person she'd ever let touch her there. But no matter how much she wanted this – and God, she wanted this with every fiber of her being – she couldn't deny that she was nervous. And just a little bit scared.

As if sensing her sudden unease, Tristan kissed along her hip as his fingers snaked around, finding her swollen clit and stroking it softly. Mel bit back a moan.

"Relax," he whispered, his soothing voice a balm and Mel let out the breath she hadn't realized she was holding. She closed her eyes, willing herself to let go.

As soon as he felt her body go slack, Tristan spread her open, his hot mouth teasing her ass as he fucked her with his tongue. He growled into her, the vibrations deep in his throat making her arch her back, giving herself over to him. It felt like he was everywhere at once, overwhelming her senses.

"Relax, babe. Let me make this good for you." His voice was a throaty whisper that spoke to his desperate need.

She groaned as his tongue slipped deeper. She wanted Tristan to push her. Wanted to feel him inside her. Wanted him to test her limits. Wanted him to claim every inch of her body.

"How does it feel?" Fingers fluttered against her clit.

"Amazing."

Tristan chuckled, shifting behind her and Mel squirmed in frustration at the sudden loss of him on her. Cool liquid slid along her ass and then his fingers were on her, replacing his mouth as they eased into her with unexpected gentleness.

Mel moaned as his first finger slowly penetrated her, easing her open. Her whole body tightened in response. The feeling was strange and unexpected and undeniably erotic.

A second finger pressed into her, joining the first, and she pushed back against him, her body letting him know that she was okay. That she was ready.

"How does that feel?" Mel heard the tense edge to Tristan's voice as he slowly eased his fingers in and out of her, fucking her, stretching her, teaching her to take him.

"Strange. Good. Strange," she groaned into the pillow. She'd never felt anything like it before.

"Do you want me to stop?"

Panic hit Mel. "No!"

Tristan chuckled and she realized he was toying with her, teasing her until he had her at the breaking point. "Good. Because I have no interest in stopping."

Mel sighed in relief.

"You're doing so well, babe." Mel barely registered his praise as his teeth bit down on her ass and her mind went blank. "Do you think you can take another finger?"

"Yes," she breathed out, the word little more than a sigh.

She felt the next finger joining the others and she bit her lip, stifling her moan. She felt so full…

He fucked her slowly, his other hand coming around

and stroking her clit and she gasped, pulling against her restraints. It was too much. Too intense. And yet, it felt amazing. Mel pushed back, fucking herself on his fingers.

"That's it, that's my girl," he murmured. "God, you are going to feel so tight. So amazing. I'm going to come in your perfect ass. I'm going to make you climax as I fuck you. Hard. Do you like that?"

Mel shuddered, unable to voice her response, her breath hitching as she felt a flutter of pleasure wash over her. She was close. So close. She squeezed her eyes shut, forgetting everything but Tristan's fingers expertly manipulating her body towards orgasm. It felt so decadent. So wanton. When Tristan withdrew his fingers, she let out a moan of frustration, her eyes flying open. She needed more. She needed Tristan.

Then he was lining himself up against her stretched ass, the silky feel of his cock pressing insistently against her opening.

Mel bit back a scream as he eased in, stretching her, forcing her to accommodate him. He was so big, so hard…

He gripped her hips as he pushed into her insistently, taking her, and Mel's first reaction was to tense her entire body. He froze, hovering over her.

"Relax. This won't hurt. But you have to relax."

Mel's chest pounded and she closed her eyes, focusing all her attention on the throbbing between her legs, willing her body to relax as her mind still struggled against his control.

"You have no idea what you do to me," he groaned, sinking deeper, filling her completely and Mel found herself pulling back on the silk holding her hands fast.

Somewhere in the back of her mind, she knew he was struggling for control but all she could think about was him, filling her. Fucking her harder. Faster. Taking her completely. His cock twitched and her body clenched in response, seeking more of him. Every sensation, every movement, felt new, exciting. Exhilarating.

She couldn't believe it.

When his fingers flicked her clit, she screamed out, her hips bucking against his.

"Baby, I want to feel you come as I fuck your stunning ass. I'm not going to last. Tell me when you're close," he bit out, his voice tight and Mel felt her entire body relaxing into the sensation of his fingers teasing her clit, bringing her to the edge.

Her body spasmed, pleasuring coursing through her, and Tristan began pumping into her, easing out and then slamming back, his tempo punishing, demanding, pushing Mel further and further, the pleasure spiraling up until her mind went blank.

She came hard and fast, screaming out his name as Tristan continued to pump into her, fucking her with abandon, lost in the pleasure of it all, and moments later, she felt him still inside her and then the first hot jets of cum as he lost himself deep within her.

CHAPTER SIX

The smell of coffee brought Mel to her senses and she opened her eyes to find Tristan standing next to the bed, wearing nothing but a pair of black boxer briefs, holding a cup of coffee towards her.

"You amazing, amazing man," she murmured, sitting up and taking the coffee from him.

Mel ignored Tristan's penetrating gaze as she took her first sip. Her head ached and she wondered how many glasses of cheap white wine she'd had last night.

Tristan perched on the edge of the mattress and Mel let her eyes travel along the hard contours of his chest. He was perfect. His damp hair was brushed back and she knew he'd already gone for his morning run. She didn't know how he managed it, but most days, he was out of bed long before Mel even stirred. Not that she was complaining. His body was a work of art.

"How are you feeling?" he asked, his voice soft and kind.

"A little hungover," she admitted sheepishly and

Tristan pursed his lips.

"You know that's not what I meant."

Mel shrugged, suddenly embarrassed. It was one thing letting Tristan fuck her in the ass and completely another to discuss it before she'd even finished her first cup of coffee. Tristan brushed her sleep-tousled hair from her face, patiently waiting for her response.

"A little sore," she said eventually.

Mel could see the relief in his dark eyes before he leaned over and kissed her lips, his touch gentle and teasing as he coaxed her mouth open.

He leaned back and handed Mel her phone. She looked at it confusion.

"You promised you'd call your parents."

Mel made a face, suddenly remembering the promise he'd wrested from her. It wasn't fair, the way he'd used her body against her, knowing perfectly well that she'd agree to just about anything as long as he continued to touch her.

His fingers intertwined with hers as he toyed with the diamond ring on her finger. "Mel, you're going to be my wife. You have to tell them."

Mel wrinkled her nose. "I haven't had my coffee yet." She knew she was just making excuses, but it seemed cruel to make her face her mother uncaffeinated. Tristan was silent for a moment and when he finally spoke, his voice was soft and pensive.

"I'm tired of hiding. I'm tired of pretending you aren't the love of my life. I want to take you out to dinner and not be afraid we'll run into someone. I want to see where you grew up. I want it all. And that means telling your parents. Because we aren't getting married without telling them. Don't make me wait."

Mel's heart constricted just hearing him talk about their future together. Tristan, who'd told her all he wanted was five days of fucking, no commitment, no future, who now so easily told her he wanted to spend the rest of his life with her. She wanted more than anything to make him happy. To give him everything he asked for.

Still, the thought of facing her parents...

She sighed, brushing her hair out of her eyes.

Tristan just raised one eyebrow. "Mel, I want them to know me. To know us. My parents are gone. I don't have anyone to tell, but you do. Don't you want your father to walk you down the aisle?"

Mel made a face as she yanked the phone from him.

"Fine," she mumbled, getting up from the bed and taking her phone and coffee into the bathroom.

"Thank you."

"Don't thank me yet," she said over her shoulder. "You haven't met my parents yet."

When Mel emerged from the bathroom twenty minutes later, Tristan was sitting on the bed waiting for her.

"We're invited for lunch tomorrow," she said, crawling onto his lap and wrapping her arms around his shoulders, feeling the comforting warmth of his bare skin against hers. She pressed her nose into his neck, inhaling deeply.

"You owe me for this," she mumbled, making Tristan laugh.

"I'm sure I'll find some way to make it up to you," he teased.

CHAPTER SEVEN

Mel didn't say a word. She just stared out the window, her brow furrowed, as Tristan drove to her parents' house. He reached over and gave her thigh a squeeze before turning back to the road. He had no idea what to expect, but Mel's silence was beginning to worry him.

"Keep going straight. The road will bear to the right. I'll tell you when to turn," Mel said, her voice a somber monotone that did nothing to ease Tristan's growing concern.

It was obvious Mel's relationship with her parents was strained, but he'd never seen her like this. Silent. Brooding.

The road curved gently around a clear blue bay and Tristan could see the sailboats, their brightly colored spinnakers catching in the afternoon breeze, as they cut across the water. When he snuck another glance at Mel, her shoulders were hunched and her eyes locked on some unknown point in the distance.

"What's wrong?"

Mel turned, fixing her vacant stare on him before

answering. "Nothing."

But it was clear something was wrong. Back in Princeton, this had seemed so necessary. It's what you did. You got engaged and you met the parents. But they weren't even at the house yet and he'd seen the woman he loved transformed into a total stranger.

Whatever problems she had with her parents went deeper than bickering over Thanksgiving dinner. He shouldn't have pushed her. It wasn't like he needed their approval. It wouldn't make the slightest difference in the way he felt. He was marrying Mel and that was that.

The road narrowed, crowded in by mature oak trees and Tristan slowed, following the gentle curve of the road. It was hard to believe they were only an hour from New York City. It felt like a different world. Lush, green, pastoral.

"Make a left at the brick gate. The house is a half-mile farther."

Tristan's eyes widened as he pulled in front of an enormous white Colonial house with black shutters and killed the engine. Glancing past Mel, he could see the sun reflecting off the Long Island Sound in the distance.

"*This* is where you grew up?" He couldn't hide his surprise. What had he really expected? That Mel had grown up in some shitty little house that she was ashamed of showing him? Maybe it wasn't her parents she was ashamed of. Maybe it was him.

Mel tugged open the car door, giving him a wane smile. "My parents are rich. I'm still just a poor grad student."

In the shadow of the house, Mel looked fragile and lost and Tristan grabbed her hand, giving it a little squeeze.

"Nervous?"

Mel bit her lip before nodding.

"It'll be fine," he said, trying to assure her and realizing he needed the assurance just as much as she did. He'd never had the occasion to meet a girlfriend's family before and he had to admit, if only to himself, the thought made him uneasy.

It wasn't a feeling Tristan liked. At all. He pushed his shoulders back. He could do this. No problem.

Tristan brushed a lock of hair from Mel's face and leaned down, his lips brushing her cheek. "It'll be fine," he repeated.

Mel stepped into the foyer, breathing in the familiar scent of potpourri that her mother had been discretely distributing around the house since she was a child.

"Mom?" she called out, dropping Tristan's hand. She'd had to fight the urge to remove the engagement ring before coming in. No way Tristan would understand.

Sylvie Potter sauntered into the room looking flawless, as usual. Her icy blond hair was pulled back in a tight chignon and she was wearing a man-tailored shirt and slacks, her makeup perfect.

"Darling, you made it." She glanced at the oversized watch on her delicate wrist, frowning. "You're late."

Mel's shoulders sagged. "Mom, this is Tristan. The man I told you about." She couldn't bring herself to use the word fiancée. Not yet.

Sylvie's eyes narrowed on Tristan, and Mel could feel him stand a little taller.

"It's very nice to meet you, Mrs. Potter."

Sylvie pursed her lips in vexation. "Sylvie, please." She

focused her eyes once more on Mel. "I never thought the day would come that my darling daughter brings a man home."

She turned on her heels and walked away, giving Mel a chance to catch her breath. All they had to do was get through lunch and then they could go back home.

Sylvie glanced over her shoulder. "Lunch is being served on the patio."

The smell of freshly cut grass filled the air as Tristan took in the breathtaking view from the patio. A long green lawn rolled down a gentle hill, ending in the sandy beach and the Long Island Sound. This wasn't just a house. It was an estate. He tried to imagine a young Mel running outside, carefree, barefoot, her hair catching the afternoon sun, but one look at Sylvie Potter and he didn't think there'd been much running or playing in the dirt.

"It's good of you to have us," he said when neither Mel nor her mother showed any intention of breaking the tense silence that hung over the table, interrupted only by the chatter of birds.

Sylvie lifted her frail shoulders. "You must understand my daughter doesn't deign to visit often. The last time I saw her she slammed the door in my face and told me not to expect her for Christmas." She pretended to look at her watch. "That was a year ago. Harold will be back any minute. You know how your father hates to be kept waiting."

"There was traffic," Mel said softly.

"There's always something, isn't there?" Sylvie studied Mel for a moment before adding, "You've gained weight."

Tristan frowned. Mel's mother was all skin and bones,

and while it was clear she'd once been a truly beautiful woman, her beauty was cold. Brittle. Whereas Mel radiated warmth. He loved every inch of her. Her delicious curves. The swell of her hips. The flesh that he could hold onto when he fucked her.

He couldn't imagine her any smaller. Nor did he want to.

He opened his mouth to say something just as Harold Potter strode onto the patio wearing a navy blue Brooks Brothers blazer and khaki shorts.

He took one look at Mel and turned to Tristan, putting out his hand. "Harold Potter, it's good to meet you." He yanked back his chair and sat. "What are you having to drink?"

Tristan noted the way he barely even looked at Mel. "Water is fine."

Harold frowned. "Water is for bathing, not drinking. What would you really like?"

Tristan glanced at Mel, but she just shrugged her shoulders. "A glass of wine."

Harold gave a satisfied nod. "That's more like it. So, tell me, how do you know Melanie?"

And here it begins, Tristan thought, steeling himself. "We met at Columbia." He had no intention of starting off his relationship with his future in-laws with a lie but he wasn't about to offer up the fact that he'd been her professor at the time, either.

Harold leaned back, his sharp blue eyes taking in everything. "You're a little old to have studied together."

"I teach at Columbia. Though I'm at Princeton this year."

Harold laughed derisively. "So you're a professor?"

"Of literature, yes."

Harold frowned and judging by the harsh lines cut into his handsome face, this was a common expression. "How nice." His gaze swiveled back to Mel. "Let me guess, you've run out of money and realized it's not so nice out in the real world."

"Dad," Mel started, looking mortified.

"We both know you aren't here to apologize to your mother, so what is this about? Money? Are you pregnant?"

"Harold," Sylvie said in a subdued voice, but her warning went unheard.

Tristan glanced around the table, his fists clenched in his lap, too shocked to speak.

"If you aren't pregnant, then what is this about? I was supposed to see Bob Hamilton this afternoon."

Tristan felt a slow burn across his face as his jaw worked in anger. "Don't you dare speak to her like that."

Harold flicked his eyes over Tristan dismissively. "Stay out of this, son. It's really none of your business."

"This is certainly my business," Tristan responded, striving to keep his voice even.

Harold turned the full weight of his gaze on Tristan. "This is a family matter."

Yes, it certainly was. Mel was his family. Tristan looked at her father in disgust before turning to her. "We should go," he said, pushing back his chair and reaching his hand out to Mel. "I'm sorry, this was a terrible idea," he said, his voice softening.

Mel shook her head, a look of determination crossing her face. She turned back to her parents and Tristan could see the tension in her shoulders, but she stood her ground, refusing to be bullied and in that moment, Tristan couldn't have been prouder.

She sucked in a deep breath. "Tristan and I are getting married."

CHAPTER EIGHT

Sylvie blinked in surprise. "Married?"

"I'm calling the lawyers," her father said, abruptly coming to his feet. He glared at Tristan before adding, "If you think you're getting a penny, you're dead wrong."

"Not everything is about money, dad."

He let out a condescending laugh. "Like hell it's not. He's a teacher, for Christ's sake! If I'd thought for a minute you'd throw away your future on someone like him, I never would have sent you to Columbia."

"Dad…" Mel gritted her teeth, embarrassment washing over her.

"Were you even planning on a prenup?"

When Mel didn't answer, her father shook his head, the disgust clear in his eyes. "Like I said, I'm calling the lawyers."

"Enough!" Everyone froze at the sound of that one word exploding from Tristan's mouth. "Enough," he added, his voice dropping now that he had everyone's attention. And he certainly did. Mel's father gaped at him, his mouth working but no words were coming out.

"We came here to tell you we're getting married. Not to ask for your permission and certainly not to be treated like this." Mel could see how worked up Tristan was as he ran his hand through his hair. He let out an exasperated sigh. "Your daughter is the most wonderful woman in the world. She is smart. She is kind. She is loving. And you don't fucking deserve her in your lives. She didn't want to come here this afternoon, but I made her. I was wrong. You don't fucking deserve her."

Mel felt the color come to her cheeks at Tristan's impassioned words. He turned towards her. "Mel, let's go home." Even through his whisper, Mel could hear the barely contained fury just beneath the surface.

No one stood up to Harold Potter. But Tristan had. For her. She could see the vein in her father's forehead pulsing angrily.

She hadn't seen her father this livid since she told them she was going back to school. When he'd told her he wouldn't pay for it, she'd told him she didn't need his money and walked out the door.

"Young lady, don't you dare walk away. We are not done talking about this."

The muscles in Tristan's jaw twitched. "Mel, wait for me in the car. I need a word with your father," he said, his voice tight and strained. He took Mel's hand, pressing the keys into her palm and giving her a reassuring squeeze. "I'll be right out."

Mel took one last look at her mother before nodding and slipping past her father. She almost expected him to grab her, but he didn't. She could feel his eyes boring into her, but she refused to turn around, refused to stop until she was outside.

She slumped against the car and stared up at her childhood home, sadness welling up inside of her. She'd been the perfect daughter. The model student, never in trouble, never wild. But her parents always wanted more. They wanted her to marry a rich doctor or banker, so she could stay at home, trapped in the life her mother lived, nothing more than an ornament on some man's arm. She didn't fault people who wanted that life, but it wasn't for her. She wanted the rigors of academia, wanted to lose herself in literature. She wanted to teach, not because she was worried about a paycheck, but because it genuinely interested her.

Her father thought it was beneath her. But he'd never seen education as anything but a means for achieving financial goals.

She pressed her hands to her eyes, but all she could see was the expression on Tristan's face. He'd looked like he was five seconds from punching her father, the anger radiating off him in waves. She'd never seen him look like that before, all of his careful composure gone in a heartbeat.

The salty breeze and the smell of freshly cut grass did nothing to ease her nerves. She hated it here. She wanted to go home. To their little apartment. With Tristan.

She wanted to forget.

Mel's eyes shot open when the front door slammed shut, rattling the windows. Tristan rushed down the stairs, his jaw working furiously.

Wordlessly, he held out his hand and Mel dropped the keys into his palm.

It wasn't until the car doors were closed and he'd

turned the key in the ignition that he slammed his hand against the steering wheel. "Fuck!"

CHAPTER NINE

Mel chewed her thumbnail and stared out the window as Tristan drove in silence, his knuckles white from clutching the wheel. He wanted to get control of himself before he spoke. After all, they were her parents. The scenery passed in a blur and it wasn't until they'd nearly reached the highway that he felt his anger begin to cool.

"Mel, I'm so fucking sorry," he whispered.

"Don't."

Tristan could hear the trembling in her voice and when he turned to look at her, the pain he saw in her eyes was like a punch to his gut. He cursed, forcing his eyes back on the road. From the moment he'd met her, Tristan knew Mel was different. She had the poise of a woman twice her age, and yet, after only an hour with her parents, all that confidence he found so sexy was stripped away, leaving her hurt and vulnerable. He couldn't believe they had that power over her.

But those days were over. There was no fucking chance he was letting them near her again. Not when they did *this* to her. How could they be so self-involved that they failed to notice the affect their words had on her?

He didn't want to even consider the alternative, that they knew exactly what their words did to Mel. That they weren't just insensitive, they were cruel.

"Mel, talk to me, please." He felt her slipping away and he wanted to bring her back to him. Wanted to know she was still there.

"I don't want to talk about it."

Tristan kept his eyes locked on the road. He'd wanted to take Mel's father by the neck and shake him but instead, after Mel had gone outside, he'd done his best to keep his voice even when he'd told him they were done.

He didn't know who he was more angry at, her father for talking to Mel like that, or her mother for letting him.

It destroyed him to see the way they treated her. Like she wasn't worthy of their love. Like she was a disappointment.

How anyone could be disappointed in Mel?

He'd never be like them. He'd make sure their children knew every fucking day that they were loved. Because he would have kids with Mel. And Mel? Mel would know his world began and ended with her, that she was his everything to him. He would be lost without her.

"What your father said," Tristan started, unsure how to continue. All he knew was he had to say something to ease the pain he saw written all over her face.

"Don't."

"You're perfect."

Mel was silent for a moment and when she spoke, her voice was a soft rasp. "Pull over."

He looked at her in confusion, but when he made no

move to stop the car, Mel shouted, "Pull over!"

With a jerk of the wheel, Tristan pulled onto the edge of the road, feeling the gravel crunch beneath the tires.

"Jesus Christ, do you want us to get into an accident?"

He switched off the car and turned to her and the moment he saw her face, he regretted his harsh tone. She looked like she was about to cry.

"Oh fuck, Mel, I'm sorry," he said, unbuckling his seatbelt and pulling her into his arms. He could feel her body trembling and he whispered into her hair as his fingers ran up and down her back.

Seeing her like this was killing him. And the fact that he didn't know how to make it right made it that much harder to bear.

When Mel finally stopped shaking, Tristan pulled back, staring intently into her eyes. "Mel, I fucking love you. I am so sorry I dragged you there. I didn't know. I am so sorry. I love everything about you. I love your delicious curves." His hand glided over her hips. "I love your mind. I fucking love that you were willing to walk away from all that to follow your dreams. You are fucking spectacular and I wake up every day thankful you're willing to give me a chance."

Mel's eyes went wide and her lips parted but he silenced her with a kiss. He wasn't even close to being done.

"I'm serious. I am so fucking blessed having you in my life. You are my everything." He kissed her cheeks, his lips tasting the salty tears and he felt a sharp pain in his chest. "If you don't want to work a day in your life, I'll support you." He felt Mel tense but he barreled on. "And if you want to work until you're a hundred, I'll support you. I'll quit my job and stay at home and make sure dinner is on the table every night. I don't care. All I care about is you."

Tristan felt like his heart would explode as he waited for Mel's response. He still wasn't used to opening himself up and laying out his soul, but that's what Mel needed and that's what she deserved and he'd be damned if he'd let his pride stand in the way of giving Mel everything.

Suddenly, her lips were on his, catching him by surprise, her mouth hungry and taking as she ground into him and he could feel himself getting hard in spite of himself.

Mel tore at the buttons on his shirt as if she couldn't get him undressed fast enough. He'd never seen her like this. Desperate. Lost. Hungry. So fucking hungry as her lips took his, again and again, her kisses speaking to everything she felt inside. The need. The desire. The want.

Tristan grasped her hips, pulling her tight against him, never wanting to let go.

Mel's hand slipped between them, massaging him through his pants and he moaned into her neck.

The lights of a passing car brought Tristan back to his senses and he grasped Mel's hand, pulling it away from his zipper and bringing it to his lips as he panted, trying to regain control of himself.

"Not here. Not like this."

Mel's eyes were glassy, her pupils dilated, her lips swollen from their kisses. God, she looked stunning straddling him. Wild. Possessed. It took all of his willpower not to ease her panties aside and give her exactly what she was dying for.

Mel ran her tongue over her lower lip, her lashes fanning out against her cheeks and Tristan felt his cock twitch. "Let's find a motel," she whispered breathily.

They were only an hour and a half from Princeton but one look at Mel and Tristan knew they wouldn't make it that far.

"I think we can at least spring for a hotel."

Mel shook her head. "I like motels."

Tristan pulled her in for one last kiss, tasting her, savoring every second of it before carefully pushing her back, letting his hand stroke her cheek. "Then a motel it is."

CHAPTER TEN

Mel's lips were on Tristan's the second the door shut, her impatient fingers working the buttons on his shirt, catching Tristan off-guard. He took a step back, placing his hands on Mel's shoulders, pushing her back gently.

"Do you want to talk about it?"

"No," she said forcefully. "Because if we talk about it, I'm going to start crying and I don't want to cry."

Tristan looked at her sadly, pity washing over him. "You're allowed to cry," he said slowly.

Mel shook her head stubbornly. "I don't want to cry. I want you to fuck me." Mel sucked in a ragged breath, desperately fighting for control. "Fuck me until I forget everything else. Take me. Make me forget."

Tristan looked at her, suddenly realizing what she was asking. She wanted him to take control. To dominate her. Wanted to erase everything about this afternoon with his body and his touch. The thought both thrilled him and made him weary. "Are you sure?"

"Make me forget."

He could hear the desperate pleading in her voice and he pressed his lips together. She couldn't bury her feelings forever, but right now, if this was what she thought she needed then it was what he needed to do.

He gave her one last tender kiss because when he took a step back, he knew had to be someone else. He had to give her this, even if it wasn't what he wanted.

He gave Mel a stern look, shaking off his misgivings. "Get undressed."

Relief flooded Mel's face the moment she realized he wasn't going to fight her on this. She pulled off her dress, dropping it carelessly to the floor. She looked so beautiful, so fragile and while all he wanted to do was scoop her up in his arms, this wasn't about what he wanted. This was about what Mel needed.

"Get on the bed."

Mel crawled onto the bed and Tristan nodded to himself. He looked around the motel room quickly and found what he was looking for. He threw Mel's scarf on the bed. "Tie that over your eyes. I'll be back in a little. Leave the door unlocked. Put in your headphones and play something, loud. I don't want you hearing anything."

Mel's lips fell open and he could see the arousal and the fear there and he hated himself a little, but his cock throbbed. With that, he turned and walked out of the room, letting the door slam shut behind him.

Mel bit her lip. She'd expected Tristan to tie her up, fuck her hard, maybe spank her until her ass glowed. She hadn't imagined he'd leave her naked in the motel room while he was God knows where. She knew no one else would come in, but the possibility ignited her. She was exposed, open, vulnerable and she could feel the arousal pulsing between her thighs.

Blood rushed in her ears as music pounded over her, erasing everything but her thoughts.

Minutes ticked by and her anxiety only grew along with her arousal. How long would he make her wait? She'd seen it in his eyes. He knew how much she needed this. Knew how much she needed him.

And he'd promised to take care of her.

The cold air made her nipples hard and she fought the urge to remove the blindfold. For all she knew, Tristan was sitting in the room, watching her squirm. Her ears perked when she thought she heard something, a slight movement, a shuffle, but she couldn't be sure.

Time stilled. And Mel felt the first inkling of panic start in her chest. What if Tristan didn't come? What if someone else came into the room by mistake?

She squeezed her eyes shut, but her mind returned to this afternoon. Her father had treated Tristan like a criminal. And her mother, her mother had sat there in silent judgment. Her criticism stung, even now. Mel wished she didn't care, that it didn't matter to her, but the truth was, it did.

She squeezed her eyes shut tight behind the blindfold. She wouldn't cry. Crying meant her parents won.

Mel jumped at the sudden dip in the mattress. Tristan's hand moved slowly up her calf, his touch light and teasing and Mel let out a sigh of relief, her heart still pounding, the blood still rushing in her ears.

This was what she wanted.

Tristan gripped her hips, yanking her down the mattress and spreading her legs forcefully. His touch was electric. Invigorating. She could feel it all the way to her pussy, making her wet and antsy. She moaned as Tristan's fingers brushed against her slick sex, his touch feather-light, designed to tease and torture.

She jumped when she felt his hot breath on her overly sensitive skin.

She was on fire. Her skin burning with need. The music playing intensified, washing over Mel and suddenly Tristan's hands were gone and she felt an overwhelming emptiness crash over her.

She needed his touch. She struggled to hear anything, any indication of what was coming next, but there was nothing but the blood pounding in her ears and the music playing through her headphones. Her sex throbbed. Her skin felt prickly and flushed. She was tempted to play with herself until the world dissolved and nothing remained but her body, writhing in pleasure. She dug her fingers into the duvet, fighting the urge. This wasn't just about pleasure. This was about letting go.

She felt his hot breath on her sex and moaned. Everything felt intensified. She'd never been blindfolded before and she hadn't expected just how much it would change the experience.

Tristan kissed the crease where her thigh met her sex, flicking his tongue along her skin, licking her with delicious purpose.

"Tristan," she murmured, her voice sounding strange even to her ears.

She couldn't hear his response, could only feel his kisses as they moved down her leg, his tongue licking her skin until he came to her knee. Gingerly, he placed her leg over his shoulder, spreading her wanting sex for his mouth. She bit her lip. But instead, he continued the torture down her other leg, kissing and teasing, nibbling her flesh, making her squirm, her body begging for more. Mel clawed at the rough bedspread, writhing with need and frustration.

She jumped when something cold and wet trailed against her belly, making her skin tighten as her mind struggled to place the new sensation. Ice, she realized. And then it was gone, replaced with Tristan's hot mouth, his touch lapping up the cold liquid on her skin.

When his lips finally closed over her sex, she nearly screamed.

But just as soon as she'd finally felt heaven, his lips were gone, trailing more kisses along her hips, his tongue dipping into her belly button, making her squirm. She could feel his erection pressed against her thigh.

"Tristan, please, Tristan…" she begged, knowing it was useless. Tristan would fuck her when he was ready. She'd asked him to make her forget and she knew he'd do just that.

Lips closed around her nipple, Tristan's teeth digging into her pulsing flesh, the bite sharp and she could feel it down to her toes. With expert attention, he licked and sucked and bit, dragging out her pleasure, until Mel thought she would come apart from just his mouth.

She shook with unbearable need. She needed Tristan. Inside of her. Filling her. Pushing away the last remnants of the day.

His hot skin pushed her into the mattress, his weight comforting and demanding as he took her mouth and she could taste her arousal on his lips, and she moaned into him, writhing beneath him, her body begging.

The tip of his cock brushed against her slick folds, nudging her open and she arched her hips, urging him forward. Her fingers dug into his shoulders until she was afraid she'd draw blood. And just as quickly, Tristan spun her around until her face was pressed into the mattress and she was breathing hard, pinned beneath him as he manipulated her body, lifting her onto her knees until her ass was presented to him.

She could feel the cold air on her slick sex, making her moan, making her inner muscles twitch with expectation.

"Please fuck me," she begged.

His finger ran along her sex, making her squirm. If he didn't fuck her soon, she'd explode. She cried out when he roughly pushed into her, his fingers stretching her, pushing her forward.

It wasn't enough. It would never be enough. He pumped into her, one hand between her shoulder blades, pressing her breasts firmly into the mattress. She wiggled her ass.

"I'm serious."

His lips met her neck, sending a spiral of pleasure through her.

There was nothing but Tristan's hands, his lips, his body, on her. This was everything. Nothing else mattered.

Without warning, she felt his palm smack hard against her ass, nearly sending her over the edge. He stroked her clit as he spanked her, his hand hard against her flushed backside, bringing the blood to her skin.

She squirmed. The sting of his hand overtook her senses. She struggled to anticipate the next blow, but with her eyes blindfolded and the music blaring through her headphones, there was no way to know when it would come next.

His hand, massaging her flesh, soothing her.

His hand, smacking her ass until she called out.

When Tristan's hard cock pushed into her in a fluid thrust, Mel screamed out, her whole body coming apart as he fucked her roughly.

CHAPTER ELEVEN

Mel slept on the drive back to Princeton, giving Tristan a chance to process the past twelve hours.

He should have listened. He should have realized that when she said she didn't want to call them, it wasn't because she was ashamed of him, but because she wanted to spare herself their condemnation. He sighed, keeping his eyes on the darkened road ahead of him.

He knew he had to talk to Will Hannum, the chair of the department, and come clean. If anything, the confrontation with Mel's parents had made that clear. They wouldn't be able to keep this a secret. Not for long. And he worried about the impact it would have on Mel's reputation once the truth did come out.

She seemed so sure of herself, so confident, as if nothing could hurt her. But now he realized just how much that was an act. Beneath the surface, she was fragile and vulnerable. Tristan could handle whatever the university threw at him. He'd tried to downplay it when talking to Mel, but he'd gone through the Code of

Conduct enough times that he practically had it memorized. He was breaking all the rules by sleeping with Mel. If it was just sex, he'd understand. But it wasn't. She was his whole life.

If they dismissed him from the post, so be it. Worse things had happened. He'd stay in Princeton and maybe start writing that book he'd been bouncing around in his head for years. His full-time teaching schedule had always taken precedent. At least, that's what he'd been telling himself. Now, he wondered if he was just scared. Tristan had succeeded at everything he'd ever put his mind to, but what if this was different?

But none of that mattered. What mattered was the hurting woman asleep next to him and making sure that she understood every moment, of every day, that she was loved. That she was cherished. When she'd told him she wanted him to take him home, it had filled him with joy. Because that apartment, no matter how small and cluttered now that they were both living there, that was their home.

Growing up in that house couldn't have been easy on a sensitive girl like Mel. She needed love. Needed support. And from their behavior at lunch, the Potters weren't the type of people who believed in such things. If anything, they struck him as the type who thought emotions were a sign of weakness.

Tristan understood that. Until meeting Mel, he'd thought the same. Now, he realized just how wrong he'd had it. Emotions weren't a sign of weakness; they were a sign of strength. Mel was anything but weak. She'd stood up to them. She'd looked them in the face and told them she didn't want their money, not when it meant giving up the one thing she wanted. Her education. All the money in the world couldn't change the fact that they were cold, closed-minded people.

He pulled up in front of the house and killed the engine, glancing once more at Mel, asleep in the passenger seat. She was curled up tight, but her face was peaceful. He came around and lifted her into his arms, carrying her easily into the house and placing her into the bed without waking her. He tucked her in before returning to the living room. While he waited for his computer to boot up, he poured himself a glass of wine. After the day they'd had, he needed it.

He yearned to crawl into bed next to Mel, but there was something he wanted to check first. And that was exactly where he wanted to be. Resting beside Mel. He wanted to be next to her when she woke up, wanted to wake up next to her every day from now until eternity.

Whatever happened, they would get through it. He glanced around their cramped living space. They really couldn't keep living in this apartment. When it was just Mel, the apartment had been perfect. But it was too small for the two of them. And Mel's program would be at least five years. And he wasn't going anywhere for the duration. Mel may have still thought he was only in Princeton for the duration of the fellowship, but Tristan knew he wasn't going back to Columbia. Not when the woman he loved lived here.

For the first time in his life, he had something more important than work. And right now, he needed to prove himself to Mel.

It didn't take him long to find what he was looking for. With a satisfied smile, he closed the top on his computer and went into the bedroom, sliding into bed next to Mel, breathing in the sweet smell of her skin.

Yes, this was exactly where he belonged.

CHAPTER TWELVE

"I'm talking to Will Hannum Monday afternoon," Tristan announced as Mel slid into the seat across from him. "I sent him an email last night."

"Are you sure?" Mel asked, feeling a stab of panic. She knew Tristan could get fired for having an affair with a student, even though their affair had started before he was her professor. They should have gone to the department the moment they'd realized he was teaching one of her classes. Instead, they hadn't said a word. It had only been a week, but she knew that didn't make it look good for either one of them.

Tristan nodded decisively. "This isn't a discussion. He needs to know. You aren't some dirty mistress I want to be kept secret. I'm in it for the long haul and they need to know that."

"This is going to fuck everything up, isn't it?"

She watched his lips twitch into a smile. "There's a good chance, yes."

"Well, I promise to love you even if you end up a

disgraced ex-professor, destitute and out on his ass. Though I don't know how I'll be able to support the two of us on a graduate student's salary."

Tristan frowned. "Even if that happened, which I assure you, it won't, I'm more than capable of taking care of you."

Mel shrugged. "Whatever you say. I'm quite fond of ramen." For a moment, Mel worried that her comment had brought up the worries that her father had expressed during their failed luncheon but she shrugged off the fear, adding, "Should I come with you?"

"That won't be necessary. Though I imagine you will be called in to talk to them later in the week."

Mel nodded grimly. "That sounds like a pretty awesome way to start out graduate school."

Tristan grimaced and Mel knew she'd hit a nerve. "I'm sorry about complicating your life. That was never my intention."

"Don't be an idiot. I wouldn't change a thing. I got you. Everything else, we'll figure it out."

Mel saw the spark of relief in Tristan's eyes and she knew, no matter what happened, they had to hold onto each other.

Tristan glanced at his watch and cursed, pushing back his chair. "I have an appointment I have to get to. Why don't I pick up something for dinner later?"

Mel smiled. "That sounds perfect. I have a lot of reading to catch up on. My postmodernism professor is quite the tyrant."

Tristan flashed her a grin. "You wouldn't want to disappoint him, now would you?"

"No, I certainly wouldn't. Though I'm sure he'd be

able to come up with some sort of extra credit assignment for me. I'm willing to do anything to prove I'm serious about the class."

"Anything?" Tristan raised one eyebrow. "Well, I'm certain he'd be able to arrange something."

CHAPTER THIRTEEN

Mel paced the living room. She'd wanted to go to campus with Tristan but he'd insisted she stay home. Hence the pacing. She'd tried to read, but her mind was too agitated to focus.

Mel felt like she was going to be sick. At the last minute, she'd begged him to reconsider. They could keep it a secret. It was only a year. Sure, it would be hard, but they could do it. And it would keep Tristan safe.

But Tristan had just shaken his head. "No, Mel. That's not an option."

"Why not?"

He'd looked at her sadly. "I'm going to marry you. Not in a year. Now. I'm not hiding you any longer. I love you. We shouldn't have to pretend that there isn't anything going on between us."

"What if they fire you?"

"Then they fire me," Tristan said, shrugging his shoulders. "That won't change a thing. I'm not going back to New York. You're my home now and you are in

Princeton."

He'd leaned down, his firm kiss putting an end to the discussion. "I'll see you when it's done."

That was two hours ago. With each passing moment, Mel felt her anxiety rising. She felt completely helpless knowing there was nothing she could do but wait. All she wanted was to be able to protect him from this. Protect him from what their relationship was ultimately doing to his career.

He'd done his best to pretend he wasn't worried but Mel didn't buy it. How could he not be? He'd spent his entire adult life working on his career and now, for all she knew, he was about to throw it all away. And for what? For her?

It could ruin him. As simple as that. Academia was a small world and this would follow him around for the rest of his career. It was that simple. And there was nothing Mel could do but stand back and watch him potentially destroy his career. For her.

Mel groaned, collapsing on the couch. Tristan said he'd stay in Princeton even if they fired him but he couldn't do that. He couldn't just give up his career, for her. He'd regret it. Maybe not at first, but eventually it would happen. And worse, he'd end up resenting her for the sacrifice he'd had to make.

Mel stared at her phone, willing it to ring, willing something to happen. Because as much as she didn't want him to come home with bad news, no news was worse. She'd rather know what they were dealing with than sit here, alone, in limbo, their future hanging in the balance.

Tristan's key turned in the lock and Mel sat up straight

on the couch, her eyes locked on the door.

He came in, his face set in a grim line and dropped his briefcase by the door. He ran his hand through his hair before noticing Mel and giving her a wane smile.

"How did it go?" she asked, suddenly afraid to hear the answer.

Tristan let out a heavy sigh. "I need a drink."

Mel watched, her chest constricting, as the man she loved walked into the kitchen and she hopped off the couch, following him.

His back was to her, but Mel could see the tension in his neck, in the way his hands gripped the counter. Finally, with a deep breath, he turned and fixed his eyes on her and she felt as if her world were collapsing.

"They fired you?" she whispered.

For a long while, Tristan didn't say a word as he stared into her eyes and she could feel her heart rate accelerating as her nervousness grew.

Finally, he stepped around her and took a beer from the fridge, opening it easily and taking a long drag.

"Nothing's been decided. Expect a call from Dean Hannum later today," he answered finally, his voice tense.

"But that's good news, right?" Mel asked hopefully, knowing there was more than Tristan was telling her.

"I honestly don't know. They haven't decided. Can we talk about something else?"

Mel closed the distance between them, taking the cold beer from Tristan's hand and placing it on the kitchen counter. She stared into his dark eyes, trying to memorize every feature, every line and crease, of his beautiful face. He looked tired. Defeated. And she knew the conversation must have gone worse than he was letting her believe.

She took his hand and began pulling him towards the bedroom.

"Then let's not talk," she said, glancing over her shoulder at Tristan. She could see the surprise, mixed with lust, registering in his dark, expressive eyes. "My body is yours. Just tell me what you want."

Mel's phone rang on the bedside table and Tristan couldn't resist the urge to pull her naked body closer to him. Reality was outside. Reality was that phone call. And he wanted to live in this false paradise a little longer.

Mel seemed to know exactly what he needed, because instead of slipping from his arms, she burrowed deeper, her smooth, bare skin perfect against his, her presence the perfect balm against the day that he'd had.

It didn't look good, that much was clear. But he'd meant it when he told Mel he wasn't going anywhere. She was here. And he wasn't leaving. Work was work. Mel was his life.

For the first time, Tristan knew his priorities were in the right place.

CHAPTER FOURTEEN

Mel frowned as she listened to her voicemail. Next to her, Tristan stood tense and still. She could see how hard he was trying not to let her know how nervous he was.

He'd have to be an idiot not to be worried.

Still, she knew Tristan wanted her to think he was fine. Wanted to pretend that everything was fine.

"He wants to see me this afternoon," she said, putting her phone down.

"Then you should probably get dressed."

Mel slid out of bed, feeling the slippery release on her thighs as she walked to the closet.

"Do you like this apartment?" Tristan asked, unexpectedly changing the subject.

"Yeah, why?" Mel glanced over her shoulder as she pulled up a pair of panties. She knew she should shower off the smell of sex, the smell of Tristan, but somehow, she couldn't bring herself to do it. She wanted him there, with her, at the meeting, even if it was only the scent of him clinging to her skin.

"Just curious," Tristan responded. "You aren't going to shower?"

"No."

Tristan gave her a knowing smile and Mel once again had to wonder at the luck she'd had in finding a man who understood her so perfectly.

"Do you want me to walk you to campus?"

"What happened to being discreet while we wait for their decision?"

Tristan shrugged his broad shoulders and slid out of bed. "That seems a little pointless now, doesn't it?"

Tristan dropped Mel off at the building, saying he'd wait for her outside. As much as he wanted to be there for Mel, wanted to protect her from this, he knew it there was nothing he could do.

She needed to go in there and assure the administration that what they had was real. That this wasn't the case of a student enamored with a professor or a professor lusting after someone unsuitably young. Not that he considered Mel young. There was something about her, something he'd never been able to pinpoint, that always made her seem so much older than her peers, so much more worldly.

He wondered if it had anything to do with the way she'd grown up. In the absence of parental affection, he could imagine a young Mel having to raise herself. Sure, there would have been nannies. And likely a fancy prep school. Not that he hadn't gone to a fancy school himself. But every afternoon, he came home to his parents. Sure, they worked a lot, but they were always nearby, always willing to take him to the park or the library, always there for dinner.

He doubted Mel would have had that. At the end of the day, it would have been Mel, alone in that enormous house, while her parents ignored her. Their indifference would have aged her before her time, making Mel the self-reliant woman that he admired and loved.

Tristan glanced impatiently at his watch. This was just Mel's second week in graduate school – she shouldn't have to be dealing with this. But what else could he have done? If they'd kept it a secret, it would have gotten out eventually. And a month, or six months from now, it would look all that much worse for them both.

Knowing they were doing the right thing didn't make it any easier, though.

Mel stepped nervously into the dean's office.

"Close the door."

Sitting behind his desk was the Chair of the Comparative Literature Department, Will Hannum. She'd spoken to him briefly during the cocktail hour, but other than that, she knew him by reputation only. He was watching her carefully, his face kind yet stern and Mel felt nauseated as she pulled out a chair and came to sit in front of him. She clasped her hands in her lap.

"As I'm sure you're aware, Professor Everett came to see me earlier today," he began and Mel felt her heart sink at the tone of his voice. He gave her an encouraging smile that did nothing to put her at ease. "Would you care to explain the situation? I'd like to hear your side of the story."

Mel took a deep breath. Where to begin? "Tristan and I are engaged," she whispered.

Dean Hannum nodded gravely. "Why didn't you both come to me earlier?"

How many times had Mel asked herself that very question? Too bad she didn't have a good excuse.

"It was all so sudden. We should have, obviously. And in retrospect, that's exactly what I would do if I had the chance to go back."

"Ms. Potter, I hope you understand that this puts me in a very tricky position," he began. "On the one hand, you are both adults. But the university has strict policies regarding relationships between faculty members and students. It opens the doors to a lot of unpleasantness."

"You're going to fire him, aren't you?" Mel regretted the words the moment they were out of her mouth, but she couldn't help herself. She needed to know.

Dean Hannum shook his head sadly. "I really can't discuss the disciplinary action that will be taken at this moment. Suffice it to say, we will consider both sides very carefully before anything is decided."

"Don't fire him. It wasn't his fault. He would have told you himself if I hadn't asked him not to. I was worried how our relationship would be perceived by my peers."

"Then you can understand exactly why we discourage this sort of behavior. Ms. Potter, I'm not here to punish you."

"Then what am I doing here?"

He thought for a moment before answering and Mel regretted her question. It sounded hostile, but she couldn't help but be defensive. She felt like she was being attacked.

"We need to protect everyone in this case. That means the students, the professors and the university."

Mel blinked. "I'll withdraw from the Postmodernism

class as soon as I leave your office."

"There's no need. In cases like this, we try not to punish the student."

"It wouldn't be punishment. Professor Ruiz was meant to be teaching the class but was unfortunately unavailable. My fiancée stepped in. Neither of us realized the conflict until the first day of classes. I should have withdrawn and I'm sorry that I didn't. I can take Postmodernism another semester. I don't want anyone to think that there are any special favors being offered, though I know Tristan, Professor Everett, would never treat me any different."

Dean Hannum let out heavy sigh. "There's really no way to know that for sure. In the meantime, I don't think there's anything else I need from you. As I told Professor Everett, we will be in touch by the end of the week. While I think it is unnecessary for you to drop the class at this time, do whatever you feel is best."

Mel came shakily to her feet. "Thank you."

He gave her a sad smile. "You have nothing to thank me for. Have a good afternoon, Ms. Potter."

Mel felt feeling shaken. The meeting hadn't gone worse than she'd expected but it certainly hadn't gone better. As she walked out of the Comparative Literature office, she felt like everyone was watching her. Like they knew. She felt the color come to her cheeks, angry that her private life was suddenly open to scrutiny. She walked quickly, trying to put as much distance between her and the office as possible. She wanted to be at home with Tristan. She wanted to pretend that none of this was happening.

If only they could go back and start over. She hadn't been lying when she told Dean Hannum that she wished they'd come to him that first day. But Mel knew that regrets got you nowhere.

"Whoa there, careful."

Mel looked up to find Tom standing in front of her, a heavy bag over his shoulder, smiling brightly. One look at Mel's face and he added, "Looks like someone could use a drink."

Mel wanted to laugh. "I wish I could, but I have an appointment," she lied. Tristan was waiting for her. Not that she had any idea what to tell him. She was pretty certain he'd be going back to New York sooner rather than later, and while the thought filled her with sadness, she knew there was nothing she could do about it now.

"Bummer. Have you heard the news?"

"What news?"

"Looks like one of the professors is getting sacked. Still don't know who. Apparently, he's having an affair with a student. Quick work, too, given the semester just started. My money's on Professor Gaskell."

Mel's heart sank and it must have shown on her face because Tom's face suddenly went from conspiratorial to shock as he whispered, "Oh fuck, it's you. You're the student."

Tom grabbed Mel's wrist, dragging her towards the door. "We're getting a drink. Cancel your appointment."

And for a moment, Mel just wanted to forget. Just wanted to be another graduate student, gossiping and having drinks. Instead, she felt like her entire life was falling apart.

She knew Tristan was waiting for her and the thought made her pause.

"Let me make a quick phone call."

CHAPTER FIFTEEN

The bar Tom dragged her into was one of those classic college dives that smelled of spilt beer and cheap bourbon and disinfectant. On Friday and Saturday nights, Mel could imagine it packed with students, doing shots and trying to find someone to hook up with, but on a Monday afternoon, it was blessedly empty.

"I'll get us a pitcher if you find a booth," Tom said the moment they'd stepped inside. Mel looked around. Other than a couple of die-hard day drinkers, the bar was completely empty. Classic rock played from a jukebox in the corner.

Mel tried to imagine Tristan here and laughed. It wasn't that he was a snob, but his days of college dive bars were behind him. Mel slumped into a booth and Tom appeared with a pitcher of beer and two pint glasses.

"Hope you're okay with PBR, it's the cheapest on tap."

"Fine by me."

He poured them each a glass, pushing one across the sticky table at Mel.

He lifted his glass. "To grad school. It's not all it's cracked up to be."

Mel had to laugh and she lifted her glass, clinking it against his with a weak smile. "It certainly isn't." Mel closed her eyes and took a long drink, relishing in the way the beer made her feel suddenly more relaxed. "What did you hear?"

Tom shrugged. "Not much. I was in the office this afternoon and there was a whole big tizzy about it. Hannum stormed out of his office, screaming. Which isn't exactly his style." He took a slow sip of his beer. "Are you going to tell me who the lucky guy is?"

"No."

He shrugged. "I figured as much." His bright blue eyes came to rest on her ring. "Oh fuck me, it isn't just an affair."

When Mel didn't respond, he let out a long "fuck" under his breath and slid out of the booth. "This situation calls for more than cheap beer. Are you a tequila girl or more the whiskey type?"

If there was ever a moment to do a shot, it was now. "Tequila."

While Tom ordered drinks at the bar, Mel checked her phone. There was a message from Tristan asking if everything was okay. She didn't know what to say, so she shoved her phone back in her purse. Everything was definitely not okay.

Tom placed two shots in front of Mel and slid into the booth across from her. He lifted one glass and threw it back without saying anything and Mel did the same, grimacing. "Oh god, that's awful!"

Tom slammed his glass down on the table and smacked

his lips theatrically. "Does the trick, though, doesn't it? So, you and the professor, I'm assuming it started before you got here?"

Mel nodded, eyeing the second shot glass of tequila in front of her.

"Well, with a ring like that, I'd expect it. Two weeks of classes is a little quick to get hitched. Or engaged. Whatever."

When Mel looked up, she was surprised by the kindness is Tom's eyes. She'd expected judgment. Instead, he was looking at her as if he sympathized. "It was quick, but not that quick," she said softly. "Are they really going to fire him?"

Tom's eyebrows came together as he considered his answer. "I mean, that's what it sounded like, but hey, I could have been wrong. I'd assumed it was just an affair. You know, professor caught with his pants down, liability question, etcetera, etcetera, but if you're engaged…" he trailed off, but Mel could see the doubt in his eyes.

"He shouldn't have told them."

"He did *what*?"

Mel could hear the disbelief in Tom's voice.

"He told them. This morning. That's why Hannum lost it."

Tom let out an exaggerated groan. "What an idiot!"

Mel laughed. "Someone would have found out eventually. We live together."

"You and the elusive Professor Everett, shacking up…"

Mel looked up quickly. "How did you…?"

Tom gave her an incredulous look. "I'm not blind. I saw the way he looked at you the first day of class. It was clear he had a thing for you. I mean, I'd just assumed it was a crush, or something, I didn't think he was actually having sex with you."

Mel laughed, suddenly thankful that she'd run into Tom. She'd needed this. Needed to let it out. Tristan's insistence that everything would be fine was starting to make her feel crazy. "They can't fire him."

"What will he do?"

"He said he'd stay here. I don't know how he left his position at Columbia, but he has to go back. He can't just stay here."

"Why not?"

"What would he do?"

Tom shrugged his shoulders. "If the woman I loved lived in a different city, I'd move. No question. Long distance romances only work in movies."

"Spoken like someone with experience."

"Let's just say, I've been there and it's not a fond memory."

"New York isn't that far," Mel said, but even she could hear the lack of conviction in her voice. She knew just how far New York was. They'd tried that over the summer and it had nearly killed her. Five years like that...

She grabbed the second tequila shot and knocked it back, feeling the warmth as it burned down her throat.

"They can't really fire him," Mel repeated and Tom just shrugged.

"That really depends. But I like you, kid, and I'm not going to lie to you. It definitely didn't sound good this morning."

After a while, Tom looked at his phone and slid out of the booth, reaching out to help Mel to her feet. "Let me walk you home. Something says Everett would prefer you at home instead of drinking with me. And I'm still in his class, and I need a good grade."

Mel laughed, but she knew he was right. If Tristan knew she was out drinking with another man, he would probably flip. And that didn't bode well for Tom's end of term grade. If, of course, Tristan was still teaching by the end of the term...

Outside, Mel breathed in the cool air, feeling somewhat better. "You don't have to walk me," she said, turning to Tom. "But thanks for the drinks."

He shrugged. "A gentleman always walks a woman home, especially after she's had a few." He offered her his arm in an overly comedic way and Mel laughed, taking it.

She was thankful that Tom didn't speak as they walked the residential streets away from campus towards her house. She didn't want his empty assurances. She couldn't bear to hear them, knowing that he didn't believe a word that he was saying. And somehow, the fact that he couldn't even feign the belief that everything would be fine made it all that much more bleak.

Mel tried to hold her head up, but the alcohol was hitting her empty stomach hard and she wanted nothing more than to bow her head and cry. But Melanie Potter didn't cry.

Ten minutes later, Mel pointed to the Victorian house where she lived. "This is me."

Tom gave her a wink. "It will be fine. Get some sleep. And I'll see you in class next week."

"I'm dropping."

"Don't be stupid. I'll see you there." He grinned before turning to leave.

CHAPTER SIXTEEN

"Are you drunk?" Tristan struggled to keep his voice even. He'd seen Mel outside with Tom Walker, had seen the affectionate way that Tom had looked at her, at his Mel. He clenched his fists at his side, doing his best to keep his expression neutral.

Mel sank onto the couch, a look of obvious relief, and bent down to take off her shoes. "A little," she admitted. The defeat in her voice made Tristan suddenly regret his tone. Slumped on the couch, she looked broken.

He'd been so busy trying to convince himself that everything would be alright, he hadn't given much thought to how Mel was handling everything. And seeing her there, he knew instantly that it was taking more of a toll than he'd expected.

"Is everything okay?"

Mel looked up, her eyes wide and panicked. "No, everything is not okay. They are going to fire you!" Her voice was nearly a wail and suddenly she was crying and Tristan felt whatever anger slip away. He sank to his knees in front of her, wrapping his arms around her shaking body.

"It's going to be fine," he whispered over and over again into her hair. "Everything is going to be fine, I promise," he added, knowing it was a promise he couldn't keep.

"Tom said they are going to fire you!" she hiccupped between tears.

"Shhh. What happens, happens. We can't do anything about it. I just want to spend a nice night with my fiancée." Tristan cupped her chin gently in his hand, brushing away her tears with his thumb. "How about that? Take a bath and I'll make dinner."

"Really?"

Tristan tried his best to smile. Seeing Mel like this broke his heart. "Really. Go take a bath."

Mel felt better after her bath. Her limbs languid. Her body warm and heavy. She breathed in the smell of roasting garlic and smiled. When she stepped into the kitchen, Tristan was standing by the stove, stirring a large pot and Mel felt suddenly grateful for these moments they had together. These quiet, domestic moments that she'd never imagined could have existed with a man like Tristan Everett.

She'd been wrong.

Tristan turned, giving her a boyish smile. "Glass of wine?"

Mel nodded and watched as he poured her a glass of rich red wine and handed it to her. "Dinner will be ready in a few minutes."

"What are you making?" she asked. She'd never seen

Tristan cook before and while she was a little weary, she imagined whatever Tristan set his mind to, he could do better than most people.

"Chicken parm," he said with a sheepish shrug.

"That sounds delicious."

CHAPTER SEVENTEEN

The week passed slowly. While they were making a decision, Tristan's classes were suspended. Mel went through the motions, but she found it difficult to concentrate on her work with Tristan's career hanging in the balance. Every morning, she woke up to find Tristan had already made coffee and when she left for class, he would be sitting on the couch, the newspaper spread out in front of him as if everything were fine.

His feigned normalcy helped somewhat, but not enough. On campus, there was talk. Rumors of what was happening in the department, but Mel kept her head down, ignoring everyone. She didn't want to be pulled into the discussions. She knew there was no way she'd be able to hide her feelings. She hated the way the other students talked about them as if what was happening was entertainment. As if a man's career wasn't at stake. They seemed to find pleasure in their salacious gossip and Mel had no interest in taking part.

Twice, she had coffee with Tom. It was a relief, having

someone else who knew what was happening. There were times when she felt so alone, so different from everyone else. While everyone else was focusing on their classes and making friends, she was biting her nails, anxiously awaiting their fate. Tom asked her how she was doing, but otherwise, they didn't discuss what was happening. It was a relief. She didn't want to talk about it. But she liked knowing someone else knew that she was struggling. That every day it felt like she was carrying a great weight on her shoulders.

Once, in a seminar on Faulkner, Tom snapped at a girl gossiping about Tristan. Mel gave him a weak smile of thanks and he just shrugged, his sympathy clear on his face.

At home, Tristan didn't mention what was happening. Instead, he asked her about her classes. There was something about the normalcy that made everything seem strange, surreal. Like it wasn't happening.

She wanted him to fight back but instead he just folded his arms over his chest and said patiently, "We just have to wait and see."

Mel was sick of waiting. Every day felt like an eternity. She knew she was just being crazy, but it almost felt as though the university was toying with them. Intentionally drawing this out as part of the punishment. And it was working. By Friday, Mel didn't think she could take any more. The stress was too much. She hadn't had a good night's sleep in a week.

Every five minutes, she checked her phone but there was still no news. She wanted to believe that no news was good news, but something told her, this wasn't one of those cases. She knew they'd call Tristan first. While the university's decision would affect them both, it would only be right to let Tristan know first. And so, when Tristan told Mel he was turning off his phone for the day, she looked at him like he was crazy.

"What if they call?"

He shrugged. "A few hours isn't going to make a difference. When they call, they call. I don't want to spend today waiting by the phone when it won't make the slightest difference."

"What do you have in mind?"

"Let's go for a walk."

"A walk?" The idea sounded ludicrous. How could they possibly go on a walk at a time like this? Mel was clutching her phone in her hand, but Tristan gently took it from her, putting it aside.

"You need to get out of the house."

"But…"

He shook his head firmly. "You can't live like this. You haven't slept. You've barely been eating." Tristan lifted her hand to his lips. "I don't want to think about this anymore. I want to focus on our future. On us. Come on."

Reluctantly, Mel let him tug her towards the door.

They walked together down the leafy residential streets of the neighborhood around the university. Tristan kept Mel's hand in his and Mel was surprised by the public display of affection, but at this point, there didn't seem much point in pretending that they were just colleagues. The administration knew, even if the other students were still trying to guess who was involved.

"I was thinking December," Tristan said, breaking the silence.

"For what?" Mel asked distractedly.

"The wedding. We can go on our honeymoon over winter break. Three weeks. Just you and me, in a hotel room somewhere. What do you say?"

Mel looked at Tristan like he was crazy, but she could see the excitement in his eyes. He was serious. And Mel couldn't help but feel a moment's excitement at the thought.

"That sounds really nice," she whispered.

Tristan nodded. "Good." Tristan paused in front of a white house with blue painted shutters. "What do you think?"

Mel looked at the house, registering it for the first time. A wrap-around covered porch and a front yard with a large tree.

"It's nice."

"I thought so," he said, leading Mel by the hand up the brick path to the front door. Mel watched him reach into his pocket, pulling out a set of keys. "It needs work," he said, unlocking the front door, "but I think it will be perfect."

Mel stood in stunned silence as Tristan opened the door.

"What are you talking about?"

"Mel, I don't care what happens with the university. I want to start our life together. I want to get married. I want to have kids with you. Whatever happens, I'm not going anywhere."

"So you bought a house?"

"Technically, it's still in probate. But yes."

"Don't you think you should have maybe mentioned something to me?"

Tristan raised one eyebrow, fixing his gaze on her. "What would you have said?"

"I would have told you it was crazy," Mel said in an exasperated voice that only made Tristan chuckle. He leaned down and kissed her.

"Exactly. This way, you can't say no. Now come on, I want to show you around."

Mel stepped inside, looking around, taking in all the period details. The molding, the hardwood floors. Tristan wasn't kidding, it needed work. The paint was peeling and the floors were scuffed, but underneath all that, the house had character and it was obvious just looking around that it wouldn't take much to make this house a home.

"It's perfect," she breathed out and Tristan beamed at her.

"I thought you'd say so. Come on. There's something I want you to see." He took her hand, leading her upstairs. He opened a door at the end of the hall, holding it open for Mel and she stepped inside.

The room was large and airy and completely empty. On one wall was a wood-burning fireplace. Windows lined two walls.

"Welcome to your new office," he said.

Mel turned in surprise. "You're kidding?"

He shook his head. "You'll need somewhere to work. And I know how you feel about fireplaces."

"How could you afford this?"

Tristan laughed. "I know your father thinks I'm a destitute professor, but I actually had some money saved up." He paused and Mel could see the concern in his face. "You really like it?"

For a moment, Mel just stared at him and then she

wrapped her arms around his neck. "I love it! When did you…?"

Tristan laughed. "You'd be amazed how quickly things move when cash is involved."

Mel looked around the room again. Morning light poured in through the windows and she could just imagine sitting here, surrounded by her books, a large wooden table, a fire going. It was almost too much.

"Did you say something about kids?"

Tristan gave a sheepish lift of his shoulder. "Mel, I love you. I know it's sudden. But I love the idea of raising our kids. Of seeing you pregnant with my baby."

Mel laughed. "I'd be a fat cow."

Tristan shook his head fiercely. "No, you'd be beautiful. I know everything is happening so fast, but this is what I want. Us. A family. This house. The rest doesn't matter. I'll take care of you. Anything you need, I'll do. All you have to do is ask me and it's yours."

Mel beamed up at Tristan, her heart racing. It was so sudden, everything about them had happened in a blink of an eye, but it felt right. It didn't feel too soon. Instead, it felt inevitable. Fated. Mel stood on the balls of her feet and pulled Tristan down for a kiss that set her skin tingling.

When she stepped back, they were both breathing hard. "When do we get to move in?"

"Someone's eager."

Mel grinned. "Why wait until December? We can elope. I don't want a wedding. All I want is you. We don't have any family to invite. Let's just run away and get married. We can deal with everything else later."

"No," Tristan said, giving a shake of his head.

"Why?"

"I don't want you to ever look back and wonder if you rushed because of everything that's been happening. December is only three months away."

"December," Mel said, testing it out. "You promise?"

Tristan flashed her a wicked grin that made her whole body tingle with excitement and she knew he was promising to do way, way more than just marry her. "I promise."

CHAPTER EIGHTEEN

Tristan unlocked the front door of the apartment, holding it open for Mel, catching a whiff of her feminine perfume as she slid past him, her body brushing his. He'd been worried about showing her the house. Not that he doubted his choice. He knew Mel's taste. Knew that she rented this apartment because of the fireplace in the living room. Knew she loved the built-ins in the kitchen that gave it a vintage feel. He knew she loved sitting on the porch at night, watching the fireflies. But he hadn't realized just how much he needed her approval until she'd turned to look at him, her eyes wide and filled with joy.

He'd intended the house to be a wedding present but with the week they'd had, he just wanted to make her happy. Just wanted to see her smile. Watching her cry made him want to do anything in his power to make her happy. To banish the sadness he saw in her wide green eyes. And it was worth it. Seeing her face light up when she realized that room upstairs was her office…Yes, it was definitely worth it.

Tristan glanced at his watch, knowing he needed to check his phone, but he didn't want to ruin their perfect afternoon. Seeing Mel carefree and relaxed. It made him realize just how much of a toll everything was having on her. There was nothing he could do at this point except accept whatever decision the administration would make.

He grabbed Mel around the waist, making her squeal with delight. Another hour wouldn't make the slightest difference. And he knew everything would change once Dean Hannum called.

Tristan slung Mel over his shoulder, one arm around her waist while he gripped her ass in the other hand.

"What are you doing?"

Tristan could hear the excitement in Mel's voice. "There's a time for questions. This isn't it."

He felt Mel shiver in his arms and he tightened his grip, securing her to him as he carried her easily into the bedroom.

Mel propped her head in her hand and gazed lovingly at Tristan. His eyes were closed and his breathing easy, though she knew he was still awake. She pressed her lips to his chest, feeling his chest hair tickle her nose as she inhaled the masculine scent of him. Sweat and sex and Tristan.

"We need to check our phones," she said, reluctant to interrupt their easy quiet but she knew they couldn't put it off any longer.

Slowly, Tristan opened his eyes. "Whatever happens, you know I don't regret a thing, right?" he asked and Mel could hear the uncertainty in his voice.

She gave him a sad smile, running her hand over his

chest. "I know."

"That's all that matters," he said before slipping out of the bed and walking naked from the room to retrieve his cell phone. Mel struggled up, leaning her back against the wall, letting the sheets pool around her waist.

Tristan returned, resting against the doorjamb, his phone pressed to his ear and Mel felt the nerves she'd been desperately trying to suppress bubble to the surface as she watched him. Tristan frowned and Mel felt her stomach drop.

He disconnected the phone and placed it on the top of the dresser as Mel held her breath nervously.

"Well?"

His eyebrows came together. "I still have the job," he said, his voice oddly subdued.

"That's great!" But even as Mel said the words, she knew something was wrong. Instead of looking relieved, Tristan looked heartbroken.

"It's good news," he said, his voice devoid of emotion.

"Then what's wrong?"

Mel had a sinking feeling at the pit of her stomach but Tristan just shook his head, crawling onto the bed, his body suddenly blanketing Mel and he took her mouth in a passionate kiss. Mel felt her body going soft under his as his tongue explored her mouth.

"Nothing's wrong," he said, breaking away. "But I've had a lot of time to think this week and I've decided that after this year, I'm going to take some time off."

"What do you mean?"

Tristan sat back on his haunches, his face awash with concentration, as if he were struggling to find the words to express what he was feeling. "Teaching has been my entire

273

life for as long as I can remember. But it's lost its magic. I'm no good to my students if I don't want to be there. I didn't realize what was missing from my life until now. I don't want to teach anymore. After this year, I'm done."

CHAPTER NINETEEN

Mel pulled her jacket tighter, protecting herself against the December cold as she hurried home. She couldn't believe the semester was over. She'd turned in her final paper on Faulkner that morning. She'd done it. She'd survived her first semester.

It was hard to believe that it was really over. Or that she'd made it.

She was relieved that the semester was over. While everything had worked out with Tristan that hadn't stopped the whispers that circulated whenever Mel entered a room. She could feel the other students' eyes on her, the way they stopped whispering and stared. One or two people had been downright hostile, but for the most part, she knew everyone was just curious. She could see it on the faces of the other girls in the program. What did Mel have that they didn't? How had she ended up with Tristan?

Eventually, though, even that died down. But she couldn't change the fact that she was the graduate student engaged to a professor.

Mel didn't care though. None of that mattered. She'd worked hard, proving herself academically and the whispers had eventually trickled off. No one could ever doubt that she deserved to be there. She'd earned their begrudging respect and for the most part, she kept to herself. Once or twice a week, she'd go out with Tom. It was nice having a friend, an ally, in the program, but otherwise she spent her time with Tristan or at the library, working. Tristan had made it clear that he could support her, even if he wasn't working, but she had no interest in becoming one of those women who needed her husband to support her. Even if that was what her parents wanted.

Mel sighed, thinking about her parents. She hadn't expected anything better from them, but she'd secretly hoped they would see how happy she was and change. But people aren't like that. They don't just wake up one day as different people. She knew her parents' limitations and she needed to accept them for who they were.

Still, she was disappointed that they wouldn't be there on Saturday. Mel wasn't one of those girls who had been planning her wedding since she was a teenager. She'd never really given it much thought, truthfully. She'd always assumed that she'd get married eventually, but the wedding itself had never excited her.

All that had changed, though. Not that she cared much about the venue or the dress. All she wanted was to stand there with Tristan and promise each other forever. Thankfully, Tristan had taken charge, planning everything, making it clear that all she had to concern herself with was finding a dress.

And she'd bought a perfect dress. It was simple yet elegant and Mel loved it. Now, she wanted to buy the perfect lingerie. She knew Tristan didn't care much about lingerie, that he'd rather have her completely naked than wearing even the slightest scrap of fabric. But that didn't change the fact that Mel wanted to find something special, something that would get his attention. Not just for the wedding night, but also for the honeymoon.

After the wedding, they were going straight to the airport. Three weeks, just the two of them, with nothing to do. Tristan still wouldn't tell her where they were going, but Mel didn't care. All she cared about was that she'd be spending three amazing weeks with him.

They'd spent every night sleeping together for the past three and a half months, but that didn't change the fact that this was different. In two days, she'd be a married woman. And Tristan, Tristan would be her husband. The thought warmed her, despite the frigid December air. The afternoon sky was grey and the weather report had promised snow.

The house was still a mess when Mel came in. With the end of the semester, they hadn't had time to unpack, much less put everything else away. Still, Mel smiled as she stepped into the living room. This was her home. Here. With Tristan.

When he heard the door close, he poked his head into the living room. "All done?"

She nodded, slipping out of her boots and padding across the floors to give Tristan a kiss.

"Food just got here. Get comfortable and I'll grab some plates."

Mel looked at him in awe. It was so hard to believe this was real. She'd never imagined a life like this. Every day was a gift that she treasured.

"What?" Tristan asked, frowning and she realized she must have been staring. She shook her head, laughing.

"Nothing. I'm just so thankful to have you in my life," she admitted.

The smile he gave her was all she needed. It warmed her to her toes.

They were sitting on the dining room floor, a blanket spread out, eating Chinese food and drinking wine. It was the perfect night to the end of the semester. Comfortable. Easy. She didn't need fancy restaurants or elaborate dinners. All she needed was Tristan, she thought, scooping more chicken with broccoli onto her plate.

Her phone ringing in the other room made her look up and sigh. It was probably Carrie, confirming the details for the weekend. She brushed her hands on her thighs and got up to fetch her phone. Tristan didn't have any family coming. It would just be the two of them and a couple of friends. That was all she wanted.

Sure, it still hurt that her parents wouldn't be there. But she hadn't spoken to them since that disastrous afternoon at their house. Her father had called a number of times but she'd always let the call go to voicemail, erasing his messages without listening.

There was nothing he could say to make up for the way he'd behaved. She could feel the heat come to her face just thinking about it. He'd humiliated her in front of Tristan, had embarrassed her in a way she'd never imagined. Tristan was her family now. It didn't matter that the final paperwork hadn't been done or the wedding certificate signed. He was her family. All she needed.

Mel blanched when she saw her mother's name on the

screen.

"Who is it?" Tristan called out from the dining room.

When Mel didn't respond, he got up and came in. Seeing her frozen in place, staring at her phone, he frowned. He took one look at the screen and slipped the phone from Mel's hand, silencing it.

He cupped her chin in his hand, lifting her face to his. She could see all the love and concern in his dark eyes. And beneath that, the anger at her parents for treating her the way they did.

He pressed his lips to her temple, kissing her gently.

"I know," he whispered. And in that moment, she didn't know if she could love him any more. She didn't have to explain how she was feeling to him. He already knew.

He took her hand in his, leading her back to the dining room and settling her on his lap, his arms wrapped warmly around her waist and she let her eyes close.

This was home, she thought.

CHAPTER TWENTY

Mel peered out the window at the snow falling on Gramercy Park. It sparkled in the light of the streetlamps, making everything look magical. She turned and glanced at Tristan, sitting on the bed, his feet planted firmly on the floor, his legs spread wide. He was watching her with a curious expression, his lips turned up just slightly. Like he was waiting for something.

The hotel room where they were staying was decorated in cream and black. It was luxurious and perfect and Mel couldn't shake the feeling that this was all a wonderful dream that would eventually come to an end. She padded across the plush carpet, coming to stand between Tristan's thighs and he reached behind her, his hands finding her ass and drawing him closer.

"This slip suits you," he whispered, his voice gruff and she could see the arousal in his eyes. Mel looked down. She was wearing a translucent cream-colored slip, one of the many purchases she'd made at the lingerie store before leaving Princeton. Her nipples were hard and clearly on display through the thin material and when Tristan bowed his head, his mouth finding her nipple, sucking it into his mouth through the fabric, Mel arched her back, letting out a low moan of pleasure.

Tristan's mouth never let go, but he looked up, his dark eyes locking on hers as he continued sucking and licking and nibbling her sensitive buds until Mel had to grasp his shoulders to steady herself.

"Are you ready?" he asked, placing a tender kiss on the hollow between her breasts.

"For what?" she asked, breathless.

"For tomorrow."

Mel nodded, her eyes lighting up. "I can't wait."

Tristan nodded. "No cold feet?"

Mel laughed and Tristan tugged her closer, until she was straddling him, her thighs parted wide and resting on the mattress. "No cold feet."

Mel ground her sex into the growing bulge in Tristan's pants, feeling his arousal through the thin material of her panties. She couldn't wait. Couldn't wait to start the rest of their lives together.

After tomorrow, everything would be different. She knew how much they both needed this. Needed to know that no matter what, they were together.

Mel bent down, her lips finding Tristan's neck, breathing in the scent of him as she licked and kissed her way to his ear. "I've never been more ready for anything in my life," she whispered, meaning every word of it. She wasn't nervous. She was excited.

A knock on the door startled Mel and she straightened, feeling Tristan's arm go around her waist, pinning her to his chest. She could feel the rapid beats of his heart and she leaned in, giving him a peck on the cheek.

Then, with a firm gentleness, Tristan pushed her off his lap.

"I ordered champagne. Get the door."

Mel blushed. She was practically naked, the thin material translucent across her breasts from Tristan's hungry mouth but when she walked towards the bathroom for a bathrobe, she heard Tristan's tsk of disapproval.

"Don't. Answer the door the way you are."

Mel's nipples came to hard points just hearing Tristan's stern command. She gave him a look and he was sitting on the bed, his legs spread, his dark eyes alight with mischief.

"I'm practically naked…" Mel protested.

The corners of Tristan's mouth curled up. "That's the idea. Do as I say, Mel."

Mel swallowed hard but she found herself padding across the plush carpeted floor. Before opening the door, she took a deep breath, trying to steady her nerves.

Standing in the hallway was a young waiter. Mel felt the waiter's wide eyes take her in. His eyes trailed up her body, finally settling on her face and he blushed. She had little doubt he'd seen worse working in the hotel, but right now, Mel couldn't hide her growing embarrassment.

"Where should I put this?" he asked nervously, motioning to the cart in front of him, trying not to look at Mel's body. Mel felt her nipples harden and Tristan's voice, from behind her, told him to come in and place the food on the table.

Mel held the door open and he came into the room, keeping his eyes straight ahead. When Mel looked at Tristan, she could see the amusement in his eyes and she couldn't help but smile.

When the waiter left and the door closed behind him, Tristan came to his feet.

"Get your ass over here," Tristan said and Mel felt a wave of arousal wash over her. The way he looked at her, his dark eyes hooded and filled with lust, had a way of making her respond.

"Where do you want me?" she asked, suddenly feeling timid. She saw the pleasure cross his expression and crooked his finger, beckoning her to him.

"This is your last night as a single woman. Tell me, what do you want?"

Mel was surprised that he asked, but she couldn't help but smile. "You," she whispered and she watched his eyes twinkle mischievously.

"Good answer, Ms. Potter. Or should I saw, Mrs. Everett."

Mel felt a knot form in her belly as she walked slowly towards Tristan, her hips swaying provocatively.

"Mrs. Everett?" she asked, lifting one eyebrow.

"I like the way that sounds," he whispered, pulling her into his broad chest, his hands roaming her body freely, bunching her slip around her waist. His fingers dipped beneath the material of her thong, pulling it down roughly. When he finally kissed her, his lips taking her roughly, she felt her whole body melt into him as desire bloomed across her skin.

When he broke away, Mel was panting, her breath ragged and uneven and he trailed one finger across her cheek, his touch filled with tenderness. Wordlessly, he took her hand, all but dragging her towards the large window that overlooked the park.

"Do you know how hard it made me, seeing how much

the waiter wanted you. He could barely look at you. Knowing that he wanted you but he couldn't touch you." Tristan's words were a harsh whisper that made the hairs at the back of Mel's neck stand on end.

Mel brushed her lips across Tristan's chest, watching the steady rise and fall as he slept. She wasn't superstitious but it didn't feel right letting him see her in the dress. She grabbed her bag and was about to slip out of the hotel room when a box on the coffee table caught her eye. She hadn't noticed it the night before, but then again, all her attention had been focused on Tristan.

She recognized her mother's elegant script instantly on the card and her heart started pounding as she slipped the card from the envelope, her lips moving silently as she read.

I wore these the day I married your father. I always expected to give them to you on your wedding day. Love Sylvie

Mel frowned and lifted the lid off the small box, gasping when she saw the earrings nestled into the white silk. Mel rarely wore jewelry, but the vintage sapphire earrings were stunning and she found herself smiling. Something borrowed and something blue.

She hadn't spoken to her mother since September but Tristan must have talked to her. That was the only way that she would have known she was getting married.

Once again, Mel found herself overwhelmed by her feelings for the man still sleeping in the other room. She slipped the small jewelry box into her pocket before leaving the hotel room. She'd take a taxi to Carrie's apartment on the Lower East Side.

Her heart beat frantically. In less than eight hours, she

would be married. She smiled as she stared out the window of the taxi, watching downtown Manhattan pass in a blur. This was where it all began. It only seemed fitting that this was where they'd be getting married.

CHAPTER TWENTY-ONE

Tristan stood nervously by the window of the library, next to the justice of the peace who was marrying them. No, not nervously. Excitedly. He was excited. For everything that was to come. For their life together. He took one final glance at his watch.

Classical music filtered through the sun-dappled room. Outside, the campus was covered in a thin layer of snow, but inside, the library was warm and cozy. He'd felt Mel slip out of bed that morning and it had taken all of his willpower to let her go. Now, the anticipation was killing him.

He glanced once more at his watch, frowning. Any minute now. Any minute and they would be tied together for life. The thought brought a smile to his lips.

The music stopped and the door opened and for a moment, Tristan felt all the air sucked from the room. And then the music resumed. Mel beamed at him and Tristan found himself grinning back, unable to hide the emotions threatening to overtake him.

Today marked the first day of the rest of his life. Tristan couldn't have imagined it any other way.

ABOUT THE AUTHOR

Katie Devoe grew up in New York City and has lived in Los Angeles, Madrid, and Barcelona. She's worked as a barista, bookseller, cheese-maker and organic farmer. Her idea of a dream day is curled up in a cozy sweater, drinking Fortnum & Mason tea, and reading.